WH[...] HOMEWARD [...]

SHORT STORIES
BY
EDWARD THOMAS

Selected, and with an introduction by,
Irfan Shah

Open Space Books

The Flower-Gatherer appeared in *The Nation* (1909) and in the collection *Light and Twilight* (1911); *Snow and Sand* appeared in *The English Review* (1910) and the collection *Rest and Unrest* (1910); *Milking* appeared in *The Nation* (1909) and the collection *Rest and Unrest* (1910). *At A Cottage Door* appeared in the collection *Rest and Unrest* (1910); *Home* and *The Stile* appeared in the collection *Light and Twilight* (1911); *Mike, Cloud Castle, A Man of the Woods* and *Seven Tramps: A Study In Brown* appeared in the collection *Cloud Castle And Other Papers* (1922)

Printed and bound in Great Britain by Clays Ltd, Elcograf S. p. A.

This edition of *Where Lay My Homeward Path* published in 2023 by Open Space Books.

ISBN: 978-1-8384667-4-9

CONTENTS

INTRODUCTION

Edward Thomas' prose has been qualified to the point of apology. Damned with faint praise and unfavourable comparisons, it has often been seen as little more than a prelude to his maturation as a poet. The writer's prolific output – his reviews, acclaimed but subsuming; his travel writing, still adored but sometimes derided by the author himself, and the 'continued journalism' that was felt to have obstructed his more creative impulses - are considered, collectively, as something from which he escaped when he gave himself to poetry in the last years of his short life.

Those familiar with his work, however, are keen to tell a different story. They point out, for example, the brilliance of his literary criticism and of his travel writing. In fact - the latter, often describing his journeys on foot through the countryside of Southern England - is today being discovered by a new generation of nature writers. His short fiction, on the other hand, remains relatively uncelebrated even though Thomas himself felt warmly towards it. And while, in their totality, the short stories are inconsistent, this should not deter foragers. There are dark and hard stories to be discovered – the expected pen-portraits of nature, as well as imagined folktales, magic realism and slivers of lightly concealed autobiography - exquisite min-

5

iatures nestled amongst some, admittedly, frustrating and overworked thickets that might have been cut back by the author's later poetic rigour. It is true that Thomas' prose – and the amount of it he wrote – became burdensome to him. It is true also that his poems seemed effortlessly to distil what was most precious about his prose. But with the acceptance of all this can come a casual inference that his fiction was without interest. It is hoped that a re-discovery of his stories might remedy this, for while we have the relatively crystalline beauty of the poems, there should also be room made for the messy grace of the best of his fiction (after all, it would simply be a case of a little rewilding).

And so, to the stories in this collection. Within these ten evocations, there is to be found writing which cleaves true to the tough sentimentality of those who love and know the land; and at a distance of years since first appearances, they are imbued with historical interest, with their descriptions of flora and fauna that serve now, as much as his poetry does, as repositories of Terra Britannica (as Robert Macfarlane has termed it) - a gathering of faded words. Thomas' images of gold agrimony, pilewort and brooklime flow through these stories like the ships in Masefield's *Cargoes*. Elsewhere, tales such as *A Man of the Woods* and, more humorously, *Seven Tramps: A Study in Brown* are calloused, with fists plunged into the soil of Thomas' South

> through thickets of perpendicular and stiff
> and bristling stems, through brier and thorn
> and bramble in the double hedges.

Mike, a narrator's reminiscences of his dog, is cruel, loving, clear-eyed and elegiac. Of its time perhaps, but also, in its fulsome celebration of bond between human and dog, strikingly modern. Single sentences disarm

> He forgave me so readily that it took some
> time for me to forgive myself

and what one might learn from dogs – of the comfort of dirt and the futility of grudges - one also senses in the stories in this collection.

While it is alive to the beauty of the natural world, Thomas' fiction nevertheless presents stark portraits of arduous lives lived at the turn of the nineteenth century and the years leading to the First World War. Simultaneously romantic and less-deceived, such tales are not elegies for disappearing idylls, or corrupted utopia. *Milking*, for example, is brief, hard, unsparing. Its author understood that true English pastoral is brutal.

And yet, there is also another, more surprising form at play within this collection, where crisp Edwardian prose is imbued with an almost ethereal quality. *Cloud Castle,* for example, is an opaque and haunting tale that might easily be found within the worlds of Mervyn Peake's *Gormenghast,* or an unwritten confection by Borges; and *Snow and Sand,* a ghost story perhaps, or not quite, reveals its dreamlike essence wrapped in a filigree of detail.

> The rushy margin is strewn with delicate bones and feathers among the snowflakes

Scholarly writing on Thomas' fiction often highlights and discusses stories not included in this selection - *Hawthornden, The Attempt* and *Mothers and Sons* for example, are titles more often considered. They are of interest, in part because their subject matter is autobiographical, and indeed they possess their moments of beauty but also their moments of clumsiness. This collection has chosen a number of lesser-known pieces. *Hawthornden* therefore is absent. Present instead, *The Flower Gatherer,* possessed of a structural elegance far surpassing the better-known title, for where one stumbles into revelation, the other glides.

And then there are stories, too, from *Cloud Castle and*

Other Papers, a volume published posthumously in 1922, with a partial Foreword by W H Hudson, who himself died before completing his contribution. A death-shadowed collection from which four tales have been reclaimed.

Selected Stories, therefore, rather than presenting a broad, sculpted sweep of theme or style, is unapologetically, gloriously, a rattlebag of brilliant instances.

◆◆◆

Edward Thomas was born in Lambeth, London in 1878 and studied history at Oxford. His first book, *The Woodland Life*, a collection of essays on the country, was published in 1896.

In 1899, Thomas married Helen Noble. Their son Mervyn was born in 1900, their eldest daughter Bronwen in 1903, and second daughter, Myfanwy Thomas, in 1910. The Thomases often moved, but from 1906 they lived in (or near) Petersfield in Hampshire - the South Country, whose landscape would be a strong influence on Thomas's writing, particularly his poetry.

With the publication of *The Woodland Life*, Thomas embarked on a career as a prolific writer whose work ranged in form from biography to journalism, travel writing, fiction and literary criticism, although the strain of compromising his artistic ambitions in order to earn enough to support a family, occasionally created periods of depression.

His sense of being overwhelmed by a slurry of 'hack work' was recognised by his friend, the poet Robert Frost, who suggested in 1913 that Thomas devote himself to poetry, or as Frost himself put it:

> I dragged him out from under the heap of his
> own work in prose he was buried alive un-
> der

The poems he wrote between 1914 and 1917 would secure his enduring reputation as one of Britain's best-loved writers. In 1915 Thomas enlisted in the army, first joining the Artists' Rifles, before transferring a year later to the Royal Artillery, where he was commissioned second lieutenant. He was posted to France in January 1917. On 9 April, Edward Thomas was killed at the Battle of Arras.

Irfan Shah June 2021

A WORD ABOUT W H HUDSON

William Henry Hudson, born in Argentina and a great friend of Thomas', was himself an author and naturalist whose own writing helped foster the 'back-to-nature' movement of the 1920's and 30's. Although relatively little-known today, his influence persists. His novel, *A Shepherd's Life* (1910) was an inspiration for James Rebanks' *The Shepherd's Life* (2015).

Hudson had begun work on the introduction to Thomas' posthumous collection of stories, *Cloud Castle and Other Papers*, just a few days before his death in August 1922. A fragment found subsequently amongst his papers was included in the Duckworth & Co publication of *Cloud Castle* and is included here also.

FOREWORD TO *CLOUD CASTLE AND OTHER PAPERS*

By W H Hudson

The writings of Edward Thomas are sufficiently well known to readers of recent literature, and much has been said in appreciation of his work, both prose and verse, by several of the leading critics of the time. As an admirer, I am pleased to find myself in such good company; but as a practically unlettered person this is all I can say on the subject. For me it is only to speak in this Foreword of Edward Thomas, the man, as I knew him, who was my friend and one of the most lovable beings I have ever known. It may be that our friendship was somewhat unusual, as there was a considerable difference in our respective ages, and we were poles apart in the circumstances of our lives. He, an Oxford graduate, and a literary man by profession; I, unschooled and unclassed, born and bred in a semi-barbarous district among the horsemen of the pampas. But there were two or perhaps three things that drew us together: first, our feeling for nature, and, secondly, for poetry ; and as his knowledge of poetic literature was so much profounder than mine, and his judgment so much more mature, I was glad to accept him as my guide in that extensive wilderness. I was not always a perfectly docile pupil, as he was intolerant of inferior verse, while I took a keen interest in the forgotten minor poets of the last century. This was often the subject of our conversation, and I had no objection to it. I think, too, or, rather, I should say I know it, that the chief reason of the bond uniting us was that we were both mystics in some degree. He was shy of exhibiting it, and either disguised it or attributed it to someone he meets and converses with in his rambles, as in *Cloud Castle*, the first sketch in this collection of papers which he himself arranged for publication before leaving England. It is more manifest in his poetry, that being the medium through which a man can best reveal his soul. And I take it that all true poets are in some degree mystic, that what we call inspiration in the poet, without which his work can scarcely be poetic, is mysticism.

THE STORIES

MIKE

For two or three years it had begun to be assumed and the probability even mentioned aloud that Mike would some day die. Not that there was any evidence that would bear sifting by one who was intimate with him. He was strong and hearty, and never had any wretchedness except when I threw a stick at him in anger. Looking back, we could say that his life's thread was spun "round and full out of their softest and their whitest wool" by the Fates. He could still walk as far as ever. If I travelled twenty or thirty miles over the Downs he would walk and run two or three times as far. For he was nearly always hunting at full speed, visible or audible half a mile away, or he was examining every inch of the path, seeking an excuse to be off; and if that was not to be found he would look up to see whether I was thinking or otherwise inattentive to him, and then, his thievish thighs endued suddenly with all the wolf, he was off at his best speed which no shout could stop. In the rapture of the hunt his bark became a song, but as a rule it was hard and explosive.

Seven years before, when he became mine for five shillings — he was a stray — I used in my ignorance to beat him for hunting. Never having thought about it, I took it for granted that the habit was bad because dangerous and forbidden, and also a piece of wantonness and defiant self-indulgence. I did not cure him; I did not even make him dislike me; and therefore I began to laugh at the folly of lashing myself into a fury at the vice of disobedience under the pretext of improving the morals of an excellent dog. He forgave me so readily that it took some time for me to forgive myself. And so for seven years not a day passed but he hunted, and many were his whole nights spent in the woods. It was he who discovered for me that a partridge is eatable in May. He had no evil conscience by nature or from me, and so was often superficially unwise in choosing his bird; he would make his leap into the hedge where the partridge lay when the landlord was only a few seconds distant. But I learnt that there is a providence watching over such simple wants. However much the pheasant screamed as it flew a few yards and then dropped with fear to run certain other yards before the dog, no harm came except to the bird; as the glade rang with screams of alarm and yelps of delight I tried to look as if Mike was not mine; the keeper was beneficently detained or deaf.

He was a magically fortunate dog, and it was fore-ordained, that however boldly he might be leaping through a wood, he was always to alight with his four feet clear of traps. Wire nooses he often ran into, and many a hare and rabbit he must have saved by first entering a snare intended for them and then freeing himself by force or subtlety, returning sometimes with the wire and its peg still fastened on his leg as an inconvenient decoration. As he hunted in his first year so he did when the judicial minds, who knew nothing of him except what they believe to be common to all dogs, began to aver that he was getting old, with a kind of smile that one so mighty and so much vaunted should be giving way before them. They pointed out that he was silvering everywhere, that his head was almost pure white, that he lay dozing long after the house was astir; but I could see no real reason for believing that this change might not go on, as the phrase is, "for ever," and then when he was all silver he might have another life as a silver dog. So with his teeth. It was evident that the fangs which held on to a stick while humorists swung him giddily round and round were now very much shorter (I concede this), but still they held on; he ate as well as ever; he drew blood from the enemy as before. If a stump was as useful as the polished and pointed fang, why should not the bare gum of the hero be equal to the stump?

Gradually I got into the frame of mind which was no longer violently hostile to the proposition that one day Mike would die. But this did not affect my faith; it was an intellectual position with no influence on life.

He was no ordinary dog. That, the sceptics tell me, goes

without saying: they argue that because all people regard their favourite dogs as extraordinary, therefore all, including Mike, are ordinary and will turn white, lose their teeth and die. In the main he was an Irish terrier. But his hair was longer than it "should have been," and paler and softer. His face was more pointed than was right; his ears, darker than the rest of him and silky (so that a child once fell asleep sucking one), usually hung down. His hindquarters approached those of a collie. Also his tail when he trotted along curled over his back and made children laugh aloud; but when he was thinking about the chase it hung in a horizontal bow; when stealing away or in full cry it was held slightly lower and no longer bent, and it flowed finely into the curves of his great speed. He was eloquent; his yawn alone, or the twitching of his eyebrows as he lay with head between extended paws, expressed a score of shades of emotion. He was very excitable, very tender-hearted, very pugnacious. He was a rough, swift dog, yellowish-brown above and almost white beneath, who was here, there and everywhere at once, importunate yet usually welcome and always forgiven. He would attack any dog of equal or greater size, and test the magnanimity of the mastiff and the churlishness of curs running behind carriers' carts. But if a little dog attacked him, he lifted up his head, fixed his eyes on me, and looked neither to left nor right, but muttered:

"You are neither dog nor cat; go away." As for a mouse, he thought it a kind of beetle, and was curious but kind. He would, however, kill wasps, baring his teeth to avoid the sting and snapping many times before the dividing blow.

I should like to be able to say that he had no tricks. The most splendid array of tricks only gives colour to the vulgar notion that a dog is, as it were, a human being manqué, a kind of pitiable amusing creature unfortunately denied the gifts of Smith and Brown. But this loud-voiced dog of violent ways, who leaped through a window unscathed, this fighter, this hunter, had been taught one trick before I had him: he would beg when commanded, but unwillingly and badly. The postman, cobbler, and parish clerk, a little wizened philosopher, would never let him beg for the lump of sugar which he carried as a daily gift: "I would never beg myself," he said, "and I don't like to see a noble animal beg neither." As for faults, I think he had them all, the faults, that is, which human beings call such in dogs — abruptness, invariable vivacity, the appetites . . .; they merged charmingly into his other qualities; isolated, they looked like faults, but good and bad together swelled the energy, courage, and affection of his character. Wondering wherein lay my superiority to Mike, I found that it was in my power to send him out of the room — as it lay in Alfonso's power to shackle Tasso.

Once in his life he became, for one hour, a lap dog. A child had just been born in the house. In the evening all was very still and silent; strangers flitted up and down stairs and along passages; Mike's mistress was not to be seen as she lay motionless in bed, but from her side came cries which he had never before heard — therefore he leapt up into my lap and would not move for an hour. Seldom did he do a thing which harmonized so well with those soft brown eyes in a face that was all eyebrows.

So long as he was out of doors he was inexhaustible, and he took every opportunity of trying his strength by hunting, racing to and fro, and asking even strangers (with head on one side, eyes expectant, forelegs stamping as he alternately retreated slowly and leapt forward) to throw him a stick or stone. Perhaps it was in this expectant attitude that he looked his best, every limb braced, his steps firm and delicate as he tripped backward obliquely, his ears erect, his mouth open, and white teeth, flame-like tongue and brown eyes gleaming together as he repeated his commanding bark. "What a nice piece of lean bacon it would make," said a child, looking at his tongue. He fought with every inch of his body, and his movements were no more to be followed than those of a wheel. His fury and alacrity never ceased until intervention ended the fight, however long. And as profound as his energy was his repose. After a fight or a night in the wood he showed no fatigue until he was indoors. Then he fell flat on his side and slept with quiverings and snuffling yaps; and even then anyone's movement of preparation for going out discovered a new fount of activity, and he was up and had burst out of the door before the latch was released.

When he was at least ten years old and looked very white slipping through the beeches and troubling the loves of the foxes under a full moon I confess that even I used sometimes to say that I hoped he would die in full career with a charge of shot in his brain. He never began to grow stout, and was never pampered; it could not be thought of that he should come down to lying in the sun and taking quiet walks of a mile or so, and living on pity and memory and medicine, though memory, I think, he would have been spared. Better far that, if he had to make an end, one of the keepers (a good shot) should help him to it in the middle of his hunting. That would have been a fortunate death, as deaths go.

But he did not die. He forced himself through a dense hedge of blackthorn, came out combed and fine, stood hesitating among the first celandines, and was off after a hare. He never came back. If he could not bolt out of this world into a better, where there is hunting for ever, yet with his head on one side, ears cocked, eyes bright, he would not be refused entrance by any quadruped janitor of Paradise. But then we do not know what stage the belief in a future life has reached among dogs, and whatever the dogmas, heresies, scientific doctrines (that the fleshly dog manifestly does not survive, etc.), they doubtless have no power to influence the law and lawgiver, which are unknown to those it most nearly concerns. I only hope Mike is — or, rather, I wish he were — somehow, still hunting. There seemed no reason why he should not go on for ever.

I tried to believe that each one of the Cleeve houses had a canary, or a book, or piece of furniture, or an Irish terrier, to slip a kind of a soul in among its walls — that is in the case of houses not occupied by persons whom Christianity or Maeterlinck has gifted with souls.

CLOUD CASTLE

All the life of the summer day became silent after sundown; the earth was dark and very still as with a great thought; the sky was as a pale window through which men and angels looked at one another without a word. The two friends were now silently walking together towards a house in the west, whose walls and lights they now began to expect at any moment in the distance. But instead of the abrupt shaggy hill overshadowing the house, usually a mammoth figure in the sky of evening, they saw a hill many times huger and more precipitous rising halfway up the heavens. It seemed a mountain forest, craggy and so black that in its flanks might have been carved the caverns from which night now emerged so superbly, and to which it would retreat at sunrise and nurse itself against the evening and the next summons. Round upon round it rose up, nodding but secure, until its summit overhung the rocky base and on this ledge was the likeness of a wall and turret in ruins. Such a castle it might have been as a child draws with its eyes out of nothing, when it reads for the first time of the Castle Perilous or Joyous Gard, set far above the farms and churches and factories of this world, as those knights and ladies are set above the earthly labourers and clerks and policemen and servant maids. And this

25

mount, this mountain forest and over-hanging brow, this incredibly romantic ruin upon the shelf of it, were built out of cloud in the violet western sky. In the folds of it, above its trees, and in a niche of the Castle at the crest, the stars came out.

The road gradually ascended, and often in the series of long rises and shorter falls, that vision in the west was for a little way shut out, and more and more the hill of earth and trees for which they were making increased upon the sky. But the castled forest of the mountainous dark cloud was fixed upon their brains and the men began to speak of it, at first in careless admiration mixed with talk of the weather, and then more meaningly. One said that such notable efforts of Nature were ennobling, that they gave a religious uplifting to his thought, that we could no more do without them than without ceremonies on earth. In the presence of these heavenly ceremonies no mean act or thought was possible, and although the time had long passed away when it was irreligious to do certain things in the sight of the full moon, yet he was sure that such prohibitions were not superstitious but received a sanction that was above reason and acquired knowledge, in his own case and doubtless in others. His own work was the instructing of young men in a craft of which he was a master, and he trusted that his power to respond to these things in a way helped to justify a position which had something of a priestly character for him. He cleared his throat nervously, and with some shame, after so pompous a confession.

"You ask me what I think about it," said the other, "but it is so very definite that I expect you will put it down to my own irresponsible fancy. When I see these things I flush and shiver, as I have done ever since I can remember, at contact with beauty in human beings, or Art, or Nature, or with heroic conduct, and then forthwith I begin to perform some imaginary act which they inspire: for example, I have just ridden at the end of a long day over endless hills and arrived at nightfall under a granite precipice so steep and huge that it blackened half the sky, and at its edge, high as the moon, was a battlemented and bannered tower. I tethered my horse to an elder that grew out of the cliff, the only tree in that barren land, unlaced my helmet and threw it with my lance among the nettles, and, not without my sword, began to climb. On my way, I passed several nests of falcons on ledges where I stayed for breath, and sometimes the Castle was hidden and so was the moon, and when I could see anything but my own hands and the juts of the granite in my grasp, it was only the swelling round tower and the moon and the banner that now and then blotted out the moon in its fluttering. I reached an eagle's nest, and there I fell asleep, and when I began to climb again the moon was behind me and very low, and all the cliff was bathed in light and I seemed to hang like a carven imp on a sublime cathedral wall among the incense. At last I swung myself to where I could walk on the turf among the yellow rock-rose flowers of the narrow ledge which no foot had trodden, between the Castle wall and the brink of the precipice. I peered and listened at the windows where the bowmen should have been, but I saw and I heard nothing. I raised my sword to strike against the gate, but without a blow it opened wide and admitted me to a chamber whose far sides were invisible, and whose roof was the star-sown sky, and then along corridors and up staircases and through dark chamber after chamber, with doors ajar, or, obedient to the clamour of my sword, I went eagerly forward, and round about and back upon my steps again and ever upward until I came near to a chamber which I knew contained what I sought, though what that was I knew not as yet. The room was lighted, as I could see beneath its closed door. Unlike the other doors this was latched and small, and as I raised my hand to open it, my fingers knew the smooth latch and my feet the threshold and my nostrils the fragrance and my eyes the fire that burned on the hearth. The setting moon passed through an open casement and lit up a little room, with an old table piano at one side and a table with a bowl of flowers at the other, and between the two by the fire a boy, standing with his back towards me. I could see only his short black hair, red neck, blue jersey, and brown bare legs, but the poise I knew at once was that of a boy whom I had not seen since I also was ten years old. Thirty years ago, I promised to go with him to rob a kestrel's nest, but the day appointed came and I did not go, I cannot remember why. I never saw him again till now. He seemed to be crying, and I thought that it was because I had disappointed him. And now I understood that it was no use. I was sorry, and at first eager to ease myself with the bitter happiness of telling him so, but I did not move. He would not know me in my absurd developments, my beard, my sword, and all the rest. I hoped that perhaps his tears were sweet by this time, and that he was crying more for luxury than sadness, and I started most silently to go out when he also moved and said, 'You have come at last, let us go.' I did not see his face as he spoke, and before I could turn and look at him — your question, Oliver, took away both the room and the dream. Now I can see the lights of Gordon's house. I shall ask him if he remembers Llewelyn — that little boy in the jersey. All those years I had forgotten him, but perhaps Gordon knows something about him. I wonder is he alive. Somehow, when I recall him, I cannot believe that he ever grew up; he was strong as a mountain pony and rash. Something — I cannot explain;

only I cannot picture the man however much I try, it is as if his had been a face and figure not destined to turn into a man's, that is all. After all, I don't think I will ask either. ..."

THE FLOWER-GATHERER

"Herself a fairer flower." MILTON.

So strong was the young beauty of the year, it might have seemed at its height were it not that each day it grew stronger. The new day excelled the one that was past, only to be outshone by the next. Day after day the sun poured out a great light and heat and joy over the earth and the delicately clouded sky. The south wind flowed in a river straight from the sun itself, and divided the fresh leaves with never-ceasing noise of amorous and joyful motion. So mighty was the sun that the miles of pale new foliage shimmered mistily like snow, yet each leaf was cool and moist with youth, and the voices of the birds creeping and fluttering among the branches were as the souls of that coolness and moistness and youth. If one moment the myriad forms of life and happiness intoxicated the delighted senses, at another a glimpse of the broad mild land stretched out below, and of the sun ruling it in the blue above, gave also a calm and a celestial dignity and simplicity to the whole. One after another the pools, the rivers and rivulets, the windows or glass roofs of the vale, caught the sun and sparkled as if Vega and Gemma and Arcturus and Sirius and Aldebaran and Algol had fallen among the meadows and woods.

Where Lay My Homeward Path

On some days the sense of oneness, of wide power and splendour uniting earth and sky, of infinite simplicity, triumphed. On others the spirit was content to bathe and half lose itself in numbers, exuberance, complexity, in the odours and colours and forms, one by one, in the rich rising flood of the grass, in the hurrying to and fro of preparation that was nevertheless not over much troubled about the end.

The children seemed to be trying to gather all the flowers. It was their way of striving to grasp the infinite. They were scattered over the hillside, where the pale sward was made an airy or liquid substance by the innumerable cowslips nodding upon its surface, as upon a lake, that held their small shadows each quite clear. All day they gathered flowers, and threw them away, and gathered more, and still there were no less. The earth continued to murmur with blissful ease, as if, like the wandering humble bee, it were drowsed with the warmth and the abundance.

One child separated herself from the rest, moving down instead of across or up the hill. Often she went on her knees among the flowers, with bent eyes that saw only the hundreds close at hand. But from time to time she raised her head, her delicately browned and yet more rosy face, her gleamy hair, that was as pale as barley on her temples but elsewhere golden brown as wheat, her round and calm yet lively eyes, her restless happy lips - and looked steadily for a moment at the whole of earth and sky, and grew solemn, only to return to the other pleasure of the hundred cowslips just at her feet, the crystal and emerald wings among them, the pearly snails, the daisies and the chips of chalk like daisies. Tighter grew her hand round the swelling bunch. She slipped; the flowers fell and not all were picked up again; and so there was yet room for blue-bells when she reached the wood below. In the moister fields still lower there were kingcups of gold and cuckoo flowers pink and white, looking as if they had fluttered down from the sky; and for these also a place had to be found. The stitchworts of a hedge side lured and piloted her to the hollow, hardly larger than a great hall, where a brook ran straight, for once in its life.

By the slow stream forget-me-nots made a continuous haze on either bank. She was now quite alone, under the old cherry tree of the forsaken garden at the water's edge. Six or eight huge crooked branches rising out of the rocky trunk bore up a dome that was all flowers. They were in rounded clusters as of bubbling snow, and close as honeycomb. The lovely freckled white smelt bitter and sweet at once. The flowers hummed with bees, and between the clusters were streaks and wedges of the blue. The child looked up suddenly at this glorious roof, and her smile of surprise passed into what would have been indifference, because the blossoms were inaccessible, if she had not caught sight of the forget-me-nots when the flight of a cuckoo that had been calling out of the cherry-tree carried her eyes away to where he skimmed the water. He did not fly far, nor cease to call while he was flying, or when he was seated on one of the alders by the brook. She looked at him as she was plucking the forget-me-nots. This narrow hollow was his room, she thought. Yet it was full of other songs. There were blackbirds hidden in the hazels, or clearly defined against the may flower or the bronzed flowering oaks. Thrushes talked and called out to her a hundred times: "Did she do it? Did she do it? Did she? Did she? She did, she did!" and she laughed. A swallow flew over his image in the water as if about to dive in after it, and then rose up and curved away. Smaller unfamiliar birds sang rillets and minute cascades of hurrying song. The gold-crest repeated a tune like the unwinding of a tiny sweetly-creaking winch, like the well-winch at home. But the lazy cuckoo was lord of all.

Now she had rilled both hands, and each time she grasped a new stalk some of the old fell out. So presently she laid them down in the grass to rearrange them. But she now noticed the tall sedges of the brook and wanted some. She looked round to see if anyone could see her doing this forbidden thing, and then went to the edge and stretched out her hand: they were too far. The water was gliding under her, flashing like brandished steel, and yet as clear as air over the green stars of its bed. Everything had always been kind to her, and this water was one of the kindest, so playful and bright, so pure that sometimes they came far to fetch some of it in a pail for the house. She leaned out, and even moved one foot as if to step towards the green sedge. She lost her footing and fell, not quite reaching the blades as she splashed. She was scolded for getting wet, but never much, and she used to laugh as they were dressing her in fresh clothes; and to-day it was so warm. ... It was an adventure. But her hair was all wet; she did not like that: and the water, though so pure, was not pleasant in mouth, nostrils, eyes, and ears, nor could she get rid of it. Her hands touched the green stars; she could see them; but the sky was gone. She was surprised, indignant, anxious to be out. Why this cruelty? It was not a game to go on like this. She was angry ... terrified ... numbed. She could see nothing but water, she heard, smelt, breathed, tasted, touched water everywhere. Who could have done it? Something is cruel! ... Why? ...She could not bear it. No! No! Where were her flowers? Where was her mother?

She rose up a little, and saw the sun, and the cuckoo on the branch through the waves, and heard the man calling to his horses in the next field. Then solitude: all pleasure gone, love, light, warmth, movement was nothing, was over there, was past, or never had been, would never be again. It was better now. Sleep, sleep. But in the sleep, songs, visions of the house, forms and faces moving to and fro, and herself going in and out amongst them, far away, long ago, over there, in that other place. She was hurrying faster and faster, running too fast for her legs, carried away off them into the air, but swaying and rising easily and more easily now. She sighed as she seemed to float higher and lighter into soft darkness, into utter darkness, into nothing at all, where there was never anything or will be anything. The mud settled down. The stream flowed clear and sweet. The sun had not so much to do but that he could wilt the flowers lying on the bank. Life went on exuberant, joyous, august, looking neither to the right nor to the left. The cuckoo called. The birds' songs became so drowsy that they were not missed when they ceased, and only its own echo replied to the cuckoo. The child's white forehead was just above the water, and a fly perched on it and preened his diamond wings. A quarter of a mile away the dinner bell at home was swung merrily again and again by a strong arm that enjoyed the task.

HOME

A little square sitting room, not very high, and hardly wider than it was high, yellow-lit by a brass lamp in the centre, and shutting out the visible world by three walls of a pleasant dull gold and indistinguishable pattern, and by three narrow curtains of a ruddiness that was dreamily heavy and sombre. On the walls, five pictures at the same height above the tops of the dark chairs, the mantelpiece and the sideboard; and on one, three shelves of books. A very still, silent room; and in it, motionless as in amber, a man standing before the books, and a woman with raised eyebrows and stiff but unquiet hands, dovetailed together, staring into the black-crusted fire. The man, chin on one hand, elbow on the other, tall and upright and dark like a pinnacle of black rock, looking sternly out of kind eyes at the books as at children. The woman, trying to drowse herself through her eyes by the fire and through every pore of her body by the silentness, yet aware all the time of the husband between her and the windows, as though his shadow blackened her instead of half the books. These two, separate and careful not to look at one another. Had they been utterly alone they would hardly have looked thus. They were not alone. In the stillness and silence, despite the walls and curtains, there was another presence, greater than they. It was London, a presence as mighty as winter, though as invisible. Its face was pressed up against the window; its spirit was within. And there was yet another, almost invisible, and as frail as the other was mighty the spirit of the one who saw the room and felt the enchantment of London upon it. Neither the man nor the woman knew what was this second spirit in their room, yet the room was its home. It was the spirit of a young soldier dying in a far land. He was calm and easy now, without pain and without motion. Only his dark eyes told that he lived. As still was he, with bright fixed eyes, as a bird sitting on its nest. One had just left him who had spoken a few words intended to comfort him; but all the words had faded as soon as spoken, just as wavelets on a burning sand which they do not even stain, all except "for your country." He had heard these before without considering them, though he would have struck the man who mocked at them. This time they remained because they instantly recalled the first time he had heard them used, eighteen years before. His father had said to him one morning, "Johnny, I am going to take you to see your country, to-morrow." His pale mother had smiled her patient, weary smile with some gentle ridicule added at these words. Then she looked admiringly at her husband, the big, gaunt wry-faced man, whose eyes laughed so under his black brows. She had no country. She was born in the great city where they lived, where Johnny was born, and she had never left it. Nearly everything outside her home inspired her with wonder, awe, or fear, and she held her husband in awe because he had a country of which he frequently talked, where they spoke a different language, had queer names, different food, different ways and, as she dimly conjectured, a kind of common life as of one big family. Her husband had told her often that he had only to take a train to his country and get out at any station over the border, and somebody, most likely a cousin, would step up as if he had been waiting, and say, with his face all cut up by a smile, "And how are you, David John, this long time?" But somehow he never went until this April. He had had to be content with talking, with taking the boy on his lap and singing the songs of his country, grand wailing songs that would often make him happy for the rest of the evening, merry, quick songs that made him tap the ground with his toes and yet brought tears into his eyes, so that he set the child down and went out into the street and came home, bitterly, hours afterwards to the dark house and the meek waiting wife.

But now he was really going to his country. "To-morrow," he said, "we will take the train at midnight, and before noon we will be finding a curlew's nest on the moor just by where the old battle was."

"What battle, father?" said the boy.

"Why, one of the old battles when we beat the English, I suppose," said he.

"But what was the name of it, and when was it fought?"

"Ah, I cannot tell you that now: it is not in the history books. But the river there is called the River with the Red Voice, and there is a battle mound. The air is so clean there that a collar lasts you a fortnight."

"Dear me," said his mother, waking with a start from her musing.

Then the boy fell a-dreaming about his father picking up mottled eggs among dead men's bones by a river that ran red with blood.

Those bright eyes in the hospital tent saw now the railway station like a huge palace, sprinkled with lights and paved with multitudes of men and women, and good silent trains stretched out among them which the people had caught by a hundred handles and were mounting, to persuade them to carry them far off into the black night beyond, the unmapped black night with its timorous lines of small lights. He and his father entered the multitude and crept in and out alongside the train; and it was very wonderful, but many of the groups who talked were talking in the tongue in which his father used to sing, and he looked up at their pallid faces and black hair and agitated smiles and boldly moving lips, and was inclined to be afraid, but remembering that they were his father's people he was not afraid, but filled with wonder and admiration. Even some very little children, smaller than himself, were chattering in that same tongue quite easily; it seemed to Johnny that they were very clever little children. How kind everybody looked now! He had never seen so many people smiling and talking friendly before.

"Where is our country now?" said Johnny, and as soon as he had sat down with his face towards the land of his desire, the train was gliding out past a hedge of white faces and white lifted hands into the darkness.

The carriage was full, and the boy liked pressing up against his countrymen on both sides and touching their boots with his toes, and watching the thoughts on their faces and the books and papers they were reading, and how they would sometimes let their books and their papers fall on their laps, and look out at the wild-starred night seriously as if, perhaps, "it had come . . . their country." In a corner opposite sat a young woman, and next her a young man. He was reading. She was doing nothing but thinking, with her eyes turned towards Johnny. Soon the man closed his eyes; his head sank upon the woman's shoulder, but she did not move, only took away the book lest it should fall, and she offered Johnny a sweet, but he was too busy looking at her, and would not take it. The young woman's brown eyes fixed on him softly, and, his father's arm round him, he began to dream; and he awoke, surprised that he had been asleep, at a cold glittering station with a few faces staring in from the platform, looking for seats. "Is this - ?" He was going to ask his father if they had arrived, but he saw the name of a well-known town on the seats and lamps and again closed his eyes; the others also had looked and immediately closed their eyes. Then nothing - tiny lamps in the darkness - nothing again - then over a hill a large moon began to light a watery sky, black cloud and blacker earth, and looked afraid of the huge world over which she reigned. Another stop, a well-known name on the lamps, and then sleep to the sound of the train expressing steadiness, determination, and content in its rhythm and hope in its speed. If he opened his sleepy lids he saw the young woman's soft eyes, and the earth now grey and not black, and the moon high, without a cloud around or below, with groups of houses lost as it seemed in the night and cowering under the trees, here and there a light burning where someone, perhaps, was enviously watching the train on its march of discovery and conquest; or, still later, a pale sky lit from below and behind, as well as from the now invisible moon above, a river gleaming, a horse knee-deep in white mist looking up at the train, a church upon a hill that seemed awake but alone, small contemptible stations where they did not stop.

The fixed bright eyes in the bed saw these stations again in their dreariness, and saddened with the dream that he now was upon such a station, and the lighted train was rushing by and forgetting him, with its proud freight of living men looking ahead towards their country.

Nodding awake again, he saw the girl eating an orange, a wide water like a sea and the pale moon shrivelled beyond it, a farm and its cattle streaming out under a hill covered with crooked oaks, and the cattle were bowed under the weight of their long horns. "It is near," whispered his father: he slept.

When he awoke he was upon his father's knee, and both with cheeks together were looking, over frosty meadows and blown trees, at sand hills and sea beyond, and on the other side at hills crimsoned with bracken, their summits invisible, so steep were they. "This is it," said the father. "Yes," whispered the son, and both looked through and beyond the mountains and the sea to their country, the country of their souls, so that the child's first thought that this was not what he had expected never appeared again, until now in the tent. When a gap in the near hill showed them greater giants beyond that appeared to have descended out of the sky, and only half descended as yet, for their

43

crests were in the clouds, the two were not more moved; they could see, far beyond these distances, greater hills, a land even more free.

They stopped, and there were wizard faces waiting, and the strange tongue that was the boy's own was spoken, and they seemed to welcome him. He began to step down from his father's knee to get out but no, not yet.

They stopped again where there was only a black-bearded, tall man and a sheep-dog waiting. They could hear the thrushes sing, under the clear blue and the lightless moon, from out of dark thickets in a hollow rushy, land, backed by the sea and the orange sails of vessels that caught the dawn. "Over there," said his father, pointing beyond the ships, "is the land we have come from." It was as faint and grey and incredible in the distance as his own land was clear and true; and he sighed with happiness and security, and also with anticipation of the further deeps that were to be revealed, the battlefield, the curlew's eggs, the castles, the harps, the harpers harping all the songs of his father. He had got so used to the faces of the men, which were like his father's, that when his father asked him whether they were not different from the English, he said "No," and was scolded for it.

The sun and the bright world dazzled his eyes. He slept. Then, a black barren land, a host of tall black chimneys between hills and sea, fountains of black smoke, sheaves of scarlet flame, red-hot caves. . . . Young men crowded into the carriage and burst out into a song. It was in the language that Johnny spoke, but the beauty of their voices in harmony made it different from anything he had heard before that day.

A marsh and a thousand sheep, gaunt hills on one side, sea on the other, and the young men singing a war march in their own tongue at his father's request. It made him afraid at first. Then he fancied that the battlefield was not far off, and they were going to it, and the song was sung to hearten a host of which he was one. He felt grim, but glad and bold as he looked at the dark young men and thought of "his country."

"My country," muttered the dreamer lying still, and blinked his eyes as the tent flapped and he saw outside the sun of another country blazing and terrible as a lion above the tawny hills. The country that he had been fighting for was not this solitude of the marsh, the mountains beyond, the farms nestling in the beards of the mountains, the brooks and the great water, the land of his father and of his father's fathers, of those who sang the same songs, the young men and the old, and the women who had looked kindly on him. Where were those young men scattered? Where had their war march on that April morning led

45

them?

A grim, black-bearded face was bending over him, with smiles deeply entrenched all over it. He was lifted straight into a cart behind a chestnut pony with his father and the man.

The sun was hot. They climbed up high among the hedgeless and pathless mountain, always up. The larks sang. The mountain lambs skipped before the cart.

They alighted by a solitary cottage under the road, whence a maid brought ale for the men and milk for the boy. They sat down among gorse bushes and ate apple tart and cheese, wafers of oat and currant cakes. The men talked. Johnny wandered up from the road with a girl of the cottage. And there with the rough strange mountain boys they set fire to the gorse and dead bracken. The flames leapt up like the genii out of the imprisoning jar in the Arabian tales, and he drew back. The earth was crowded with little flickering plants of fire spreading this way and that. Huge whirls and rounds of the yellow-white smoke soared up against the milky sky. The smell of the smoke heated by fire and sun was delicious. When the earth was black they moved on, while some sent the grey boulders galloping downward till they bounded over the road with a hero leap, and struck sparks out of other boulders or plunged into the gorse. The boys roared, the girls shrieked. All dis-

appeared. But all day they could see the smoke of one con-
flagration pouring upwards before the wind in a great river,
lost awhile in the hollows, seen again continually surging
towards the high crests mile after mile, like a gigantic en-
gine smoking wildly over the wilds.

Outside one cottage there stood a little old man, na-
ked to the waist, washing himself and talking to three foxes
chained up to a shed. The foxes seemed to understand his
tongue and he theirs, and neither heeded the cart as it drove
on. And now, careless of waterfalls thundering among low
woods beneath the road, of flames and smoke clouds hunting upwards over the moor, and of mountains such as he
had dreamed lying across their course a day ahead, Johnny
fell asleep, content, not even rousing himself to make sure
whether that was the cuckoo he heard upon the hillside.

The dream of the fixed open eyes wreathed and wavered. Was it the same day - it was morning and about
noon - when he stood by the door of a long white inn
fronting the sun? The wide courtyard, bounded on one side
by the road and on the other by a green hedge, was dotted
with fowls pecking idly or lying down. In the midst rose a
brown oak, very thick and stiff and well stricken in years,
and at its side a very tall gentleman with a fishing-rod was
mounting a trap; and the boy watching him and thinking
of his wealth and happiness was happier than he. On the

47

hot white pavement by the door all the dogs were lazy in the sun. Each one, except the big, smooth pointer, had a bone, and each snarled as the pointer strolled past. There was a greyhound, a spaniel, a sheep-dog with one eye almost white, a mongrel, resembling both the spaniel and the pointer, and a fox-hound. From time to time the spaniel's puppies pure spaniels broke in among the fowls, and the mother raised her head and left the bone under her paws until the pointer re-appeared. It seemed to Johnny that the sun was always full upon that white inn, that the dogs were always lying down there in the sun, and that it had been so and would be so for all time. He longed to have an inn with a white wall facing the sun, and many dogs to take the sun upon the pavement in front. The fisherman drove away.

The father and son walked in a solitary wood upon the side of a steep hill, and at the foot of it was a green vale that wound with the windings of a broad stream running fast, and at the top of the hill, where it was a precipice, hung a castle with trees growing in its crevices, and its windows looked out through ivy thicker than its vast walls down at several miles of the green vale on either hand, at the sun-bathed gloom of the oakwoods of the opposite slope, at the other castles, bleached crags which could be recognised as the work of men only because they were even bolder and more gaunt than the natural crags round about. Sometimes it rained, sometimes the sun shone, and the father and son were glad of both as they gathered blue violets and white sorrel in the dripping and glistening woods. Under the castle wall they sat down, and the father brought out a book and read: "King Arthur was at Caerlleon upon Usk ..." and Johnny began to think of bowmen shooting through the ivy about the windows, of king and queen walking in the grassy courts within the walls, whose roof was the sky. His father told him that the book was written by his countrymen about the heroes of his country, and the child made over to those heroes the glories that had once been Aladdin's, and the Marsh King's, and King Solomon's. . . .

The dark eyes gleamed like a thrush's upon her nest when she is watched.

They saw more mountains, and the cart creeping over them and among them, small as a stone upon the road. And by and by they got down by a brook and began to travel upward towards the source. There were clear and dark pools in the brook where the trout darted and the man with them said: "The fish runs away, who knows that man has sinned." They were among steep woods of oak trees as dense almost as grass, all twisted and grey as if made of stone and very old, but based in greenest leaves and flowers of white, of gold, of golden green. The blackbird sang, and the brook gushed, but they did not speak, except that as they left, the

49

strange man said: "This is the Castle of Leaves." Now, there was no longer a path, and the way was over whistling dead grass and grey stones, like ruins of a palace that must have been lofty as the heavens, and when they had gone further still the man said it was "The Castle of the Wind." And now the mist washed over all and hid everything but silvered stones and dead grass blades underfoot, and the rain that was like bent grass blades of crystal, through which for a moment a sheep crept up and crept away again, or a hare, grey as the grass, but blackened as if by fire, leaped up and dived into the wind, the mist, and the rain. Stumbling still among the ruins of the wind's castle, they continued to climb, until the rocks, now tall as a man and so dense that some had to be scaled, came to an end at the shore of a lake which they surrounded "The Shepherd's Lake." The cry of a raven repeated at intervals from the same spot high up above told them that the mountains rose higher yet and in a precipice. The boy sat upon a rock while the two men went out of sight to the other side; his father to bathe, as he had done twenty years before when a young man. The wind hissed as through closed lips and jagged teeth. The mist wavered over the polished ripples of the lake that resembled a broad and level courtyard of glass among the rough hills. The men were silent, and the sounds of their footsteps were caught up and carried away in the wind.

The boy was thoughtless and motionless, with a pleasure that was astonished at itself. He could not have told how long he had been staring at nothing over the lake when, at his feet, his father's head was thrust up laughing out of the water, turned with a swirl, and disappeared again into the mist. He had not ceased to try to disentangle that head from the mist when once more he heard that wailing song that used to make his father so glad, and he himself sang back such words as, without knowing their meaning, he remembered; his brain full of the mists, the mountains, the rivers, the fire in the fern, the castles, the knights, the kings and queens, the mountain boys at cricket, the old man with the foxes, the inn dogs lying in the sun . . . the sun . . . the mist ... his country . . . not the country he had fought for ... the country he was going to, up and up and over the mountains, now that he was dying . . . now that he was dead.

SEVEN TRAMPS: A STUDY IN BROWN

We were a close-knit and easily divisible covey of seven tramps — a woman, two boys and a girl, and three men; there was, too, an ass, but he was a gentleman and had belonged to a great house that lay near our path one summer night. We were the most dirty of mankind. No tramp ever joined us, except one, who was an artist. He painted us and said that we might have belonged to the middle ages. "Yes," said one, demanding ale, "we have known better times." We thought ourselves honest tramps; for we never robbed a poor man, not even the artist, who had art in his head instead of brains. He could not paint dirt, he confessed, and he unscrupulously invented and painted a sash on the girl of eight, so that she cried when she felt in vain for the pleasant crimson thing.

This girl was our only burden; she was like a doll some child has defaced, and had a thin, coughing laugh that went into my heart like a needle at times.

The two boys were in place of a dog. They could clean a copse of pheasants' eggs, or mind the camp. The arm of one of them, "Snag," would go through a letter box, a natural gift which he never abused. They lived more wildly than we, having come to us from a London working family, as apprentices or "halves." The elder, "Hag," was sometimes called grandfather; when he had been drinking, he looked older than anyone I have ever seen.

Of Nell, the woman, it is hard to say anything except that she was a woman and could weep. She bore children who died, and helped the ass up hill. She "married" Tim when she was seventeen, a gay dairy beauty from Devon; but when she was twenty she was "that ugly that to see her when she got up in the morning was a curse." She was foolish when drunk, mad when sober, and talked continually at the top note of tragical expression. None was more cruel to her child than she. Our cruelty, which I confess was great, she rather encouraged. I hear her laugh sometimes; it *walks* in the winter evenings and is all that is left of her now that she is dead. But she alone was kind to the girl, and should any other use endearments towards the child she became a fury. She practised kindness as a secret indulgence; I have overheard her making the child shriek with her desperate caress. I have said that she was a woman, mainly because she re-arranged her rags with coquettish assiduity; her face was not that of a woman so much as of a type that had been created by an artist in love with mere despair.

Her husband, a brown, haystack man, had an almost romantic interest in female beauty. Chamber maids, barmaids, and sporting women, he worshipped, and would consequently attend at meets of hounds. The white skirts and well polished boots of servants raised his speech to rhapsody. Yet he cared for his wife and beat her only during periods of very good or very bad fortune. He could snare a bird or rabbit exquisitely, and a certain pedantic hate of careless work sometimes left us supperless. Had he been clean I should have said there was a polish in his ways. "Not a pigeon, your honour; 'twas a handsome cock pheasant," was his scrupulous interjection in court. I believe he gloried in the name of tramp and could have confounded a clever man by a favourable comparison of his profession with the rest. "A quart of six on a wet night — a strange, neat girl in a long, long lane — to knock your man down — to have a bonny child on your knee on Christmas day" — such was his ode to life.

"Partridge" could make the most superior farmer or gamekeeper impotently ridiculous by touching his cap and keeping within the letter of respect. The finesse of insult and abjection were his life-study. He was master of all the arts of eloquence that are not in Cicero. For he had been a waiter and was a linen-draper's son. But I will not attempt to put his eloquence in print lest I should prove him to have been second-rate. According to our standard he was the gentleman of us all. He stood five immaterial feet high; grasped an oak wand taller than himself; and wore his hair over his face. I value his memory for the way he had of ca-

joling the basest of men, all the while looking like an early
Czar. . . He had the brow of a great man, a singular thing.
Of old the brow made the man and the God. It was his natural gonfanon — the brow of Jupiter — of Aphrodite — of
Plato — of Augustus — was for centuries an altar where
human thoughts and dreams did reverence. The history of
sculpture is a *te deum laudamus* to the brow. Now the soul
has descended a step of the temple and dwells in the eyes.
On the stock exchange, in parliament, in the army and in
literature, victory is won by the eyes. "Partridge" had that
calm and ample span of curving bone, but his eyes slept,
and he was a failure. Having once caught a partridge, the
accident was considered apt to give him the name by which
he was known.

As for "Mud" (short for Muddle), he was a poor human creature, and a tramp by accident. He would never tell
the facts of his early life, though his way and conversation
made them a subject for secure surmise. He had left his
own class and become a labourer. His health failing, he had
taken to the road with no certain aim. After spending his
money unadventurously he lay dying when we passed near,
and Nell lifted him on to the ass and made him one of us.
He recovered, but always seemed to be dying; his voice was
a long sigh; yet was he the happiest of us all. I have heard
him utter sour words, only against "the rich," "the world,"

and "men," who were the mainstay of his incurable pessimism of thought. His behaviour with men and women belied the theory of this gentle optimist in practice. Should any decisive political or social movement stir the world, he would not fail to point out its anti-human tendency, its trifling probable influence upon the sum of things. But the man — the politician or agitator at the helm — even if he happened to be well-fed, attracted his sympathy at once: he would insist on the man's character as a man, and on the way in which every man's actions when extended out of the reach of his sight will vary from their original cast. I believe he was an idealist. He spent whole days in searching for straight hazels in the copses and returned with a bundle like Jupiter's quiverful of lightning. "I tried to get them perfectly straight," he explained. He seemed in truth to have in his mind a long shelf of platonic ideas, dusty, rusted, moth-eaten by sorrow and the ills of the body. To these he referred all he saw in real life. His ideas were castles, Dulcineas, Micomiconas; and since he rarely met anything better than a Maritornes, his dull sight — or perhaps his charity — raised up the hands of these mortal, rotten things to his cobwebs and his gods, associating them. He would single out some poor house or inn, some unlucky girl's face, and transfer to them the glowing sentiments which he had once reserved for his inner, ideal vision of these things. He saw a miracle where there was in truth but a second-rate dawn. He felt an enchantment when everybody else felt cold. He thought that the ways of a tramp sorted better with the history of mankind than any other. Responsibilities and duties he had, but should he perish none would suffer. The responsibilities were co-terminous with the length of life which chance had planned for him. Nomadic, unencumbered by property, relatives, or social status, he was a creature in keeping with an unaccountable world. No storm, no social disaster, no philosopher or tyrant concerned him save as a spectacle. The stars in their courses were not more serene, more lonely than he. Such a friend of night was he, the stars were nearer to him than man. "If only they would warm my hands!" he cried. When the north wind blew, it killed someone's sheep, broke windows, laid the corn; his ears tingled, he grew silent, and I believe that he rode upon the wind as happily as a witch or a brown leaf. A noble sound, the sight of the sea, or the perfume of a lane — "I eat and drink them," said he. Thus he seemed to me the half, as it were the female half, of the greatest poet that ever did not live. By difficult ways and strange, such a man is made a poet. He was once narrating the wonders of an evening in a wood; he paused and paused as I became expectant, and at last said with some shame that the very trees were "like a church full of men when the organ begins; and I was no better than any one of them." In outward appearance he was, like the other six, a brown tramp.

A MAN OF THE WOODS

Long years of soldiering, tilling the soil, game-keeping, and poaching o' nights, moulded our man of the woods to what we find him now in a hale, iron old age. In the education of such a man, not one of these elements could have been spared; all will be found deeply essential. Without the drill and exposure of a soldier's life, his back would never have been so straight, nor his step so true, nor his eye so instantly correct; and it again gave him an insight, also, into phases of life on which he will begin to dwell, in a chattering senility, when sermons are uttered more and more frequently from the grandfather's chair. Tilling the soil was slow, certain preparation for the interchangeable crafts of poacher and gamekeeper. It was then that, in the lengthened dinner-hours under the summer sky, he could glean unutterable lore of the hare and his many ways. Partridges nested in his master's fields, and it needed no more than ordinary care to mark their lines of travel, their hours of home-coming and outgoing, and their favoured corners when the coveys packed in the time of the ripening hazel-nuts. At odd hours, in his tiny youth, opportunities were his to learn something of the economies of the smaller wild things of the hedgerows and leas; the thronging of strange racketing birds to the red October hips — these, the fieldfares, he called "felts" — and the advent of the nightingale in earliest April to the spinney or the hazel-nook. He had been something of a favourite with the hunt; received valuable commissions which kept him in silent places, where the only stir was the "rattle" which he whirled to turn the followed fox from a known retreat of his that could not be blocked. There, with occasions innumerable, answered by desires, he learned much, and reasoned, too, in his unguided way, and developed a tenderness towards wild creatures which was often in contrast with freaks of heedlessness. This tenderness stays with him now; he remembers the caged dormouse clicking for food over him, even in his nightly armchair. Keepering and poaching rank together in his education. Both gave him intricacies of knowledge in woodcraft that are impossible otherwise. Had he been a worse keeper, he would never have made so good a poacher; a worse poacher, and he were a useless keeper. Education, and "better manners," he will say, have been the means of reducing the frequency of poaching, or, at least of the loud, bold poaching which he knew — desperate attacks of desperate men. Many such he recalls when the price of bread was high and wages low; cruel times for his class, he moans yet. Then a certain moodiness took hold of the cottagers; a dull, stubborn carelessness; and murderous affrays were the results. Such times have gone, he thinks, like the coast-war with smugglers. It is a memory of his that banded labourers in the cold winters of the years of the Crimea attacked the game woods. The raids called for unusual preparations against their success, and keepers sat or stood up in the covers all night in silence behind suspended sacks as protection from the wind. Nights like these ruined and bowed many good men.

Picture him in his woods; for he has been a man of the woods all his life, and is so yet. Wild, full locks whiten his brown neck and cheeks; a beard graces his chin. His eyes have the cold pale-blue brightness, suggestive of weak or short sight, which is almost always noticeable in men whose eyes are much used out of doors. The power of these eyes is genius, or instinct; their characteristic is that they realize everything in their sweep, noting details which ordinary vision would not appreciate or be conscious of. His gaze is inevitably and surely arrested by whatsoever moves within his ken; he knows that the rush-tufts dappling the hills are not the hares he seeks, but he also knows that they are rush-tufts; nothing can escape him, and he makes certain, by an unconscious effort, of all he sees. Yet his glance is as rapid as possible; taking in, using or rejecting, what he sees, is the work of an inappreciable moment of time. He is little above the middle height, but his straight build gives him the appearance of being taller, and makes him what he is, a powerful man, whose strength is accompanied by agility, weight by speed. He has always been a runner; boasts, too, of his father's prowess across country. And one of the signs of his own enduring strength is that his breath is still good; he can run, if necessary, and mount the Downs, or climb a pollard-willow yet. He may tell you that "the rheumatics" trouble him, but we find how much that means in a long tramp in the nutting season, up and down, over brooks and ha-has: then he is the last to complain, for the excitement of youth over the gipsying is as strong as ever in him. His dress, though he knows it not, by a curious but natural adaptation to surroundings, has become of unspeakable hues; slowly he has taken the colours of the wildwood in autumn's grey and brown, like the lizard in its native fern and parched rock or sward. Reminiscences of bird's-nesting raids are about him; undoubted evidences of his trespassing, in the stains of the keeper's "tar trap"; sand, from the quarries, where an owl occupied two martins' tunnels whose partition slipped; lichen from the oaks, and green mould from the beeches where we sup. Many, many colours impress his sunburnt coat, his hat no less; unlike the Downs of his nativity, his cloth has emeralded in the sunshine.

He is a sportsman, with knowledge of a gun, but a better poacher, we confess; a fisherman, who can bait a hook, yet a better "tickler" of tench and trout. In fishing he shows a failing that is often conspicuous in men used, as he is, to other methods and waters; he has too much slow patience — fonder, with rod in hand, of a joke than of his sport, and of the moorhen paddling than of either; he will sit for hours with no encouragement but "something in the air" to keep him at his work. David is a naturalist, yet something of a quack — knows and loves the gold agrimony wand or the pilewort, February's star, but fears nightshade and brooklime more. On the subject of herbs, he is, of course, superstitiously old-fashioned, daring not to doubt; to him they are infallible. The same reverence for the sweet, small gifts of Nature makes him over-ready oftentimes to find "Tongues in trees, books in the running brooks; Sermons in stones, and good in everything." His "tongues," there found, are too often dumb or vain; his "books" might be deemed idle; but good he does find, and communicates with rare simplicity. His love of the greenwood is, in very fact, deep-seated. The superstition of our man of the woods with regard to herbs is allied to his speculation about birds; but it is only the speculation of almost all dwellers in the country. Just as the old people know there are tree magpies, and bush magpies, so he will have it that the "twink" is other than the "piefinch"; yet his twink, evidently named from the chaffinch's cry, makes a similar nest to the pief-inch, and is as dainty in its use of lichen. "Piefinch" is a common West Country name for the chaffinch. The songs, the call-notes, the flights, the habits, sociable or solitary, of wild birds are known to him. His imitations of the cries of woodlanders and birds of the field are exquisitely close; their consummation is in his rendering of the bullfinch's melancholy "pipe," and of the young rook's clamour, swallowing a worm.

The old man's vocabulary is mixed and strange; many of its words being untraceable, most of them derived from contact with the wandering gipsies. He knows something of Romany, and speaks of the "Diddikai," as he correctly calls him, or half-bred gipsy, as more dangerous and fierce than the rest. David, the old poacher and soldier, "traveller" once, perchance, is keen-witted and thoughtful; at times a light smile plays gracefully about the wrinkles of time and trouble in his cheek. At night, when he gathers his boys about him, there is grave talk and bandied jest, and thrusts of wit. Perhaps in the midst of the "godship" one is ailing, and inevitably he suffers doctoring with long, dark, bitter draughts of mysterious tea.

MILKING

The end of April was sappy, careless, and profuse. One day it was all eagerness and energy and gave no rest to the wind and the sun, on the earth or in the waters or in the clouds of the sky, and the songs of the birds were a mad medley. Another day it was indolent: a soft grey sky without form covered all; there was no wind; the birds were still ; the lusty, buxom spring, a pretty and merry slut, with her sleeves and skirts tucked up and her hair down over her eyes and shoulders, had fallen asleep in the midst of her toil and nothing could waken her but a thunderstorm in the night. The next day she was simply at play with showers and sunlight, sunlight and showers, at play with sky and earth as if they were but coloured silks and now she fluttered the white and blue and green together and then, wearying of that, held up the grey and the grey-white and the green, and lastly mingled all together inextricably. For the most part she preferred not to let either go quite out of sight; when the heavy rain fell on the rustling wood it was out of a sky serene, lustrous, and mild; and when the light was steady and the rain tripping away from it upon myriad feet down among the leaves to the earth, still the shadows of the rain clouds stole over the hills like smoke. There was a gamesome spirit abroad. It was seen in the amorous conflict of rain and sun, and heard in the cry of the titmouse along the hedge: "Fitchy! fitchy!"

Rain or not, always far away in the south there was a cluster of white peaks apparently belonging to a land that knew neither our sun nor our rain. Rain or sunshine or both made little difference to the shed at the cross roads. It was shadowy and old under a roof that was patched and hollowed like the sail of a ship. The door was open, but on either side the piles of dung were high and long and allowed the sun to enter the shed only for half an hour each day. And now in that half-hour the farmer Weekes was going to milk the last of his seven cows. Until now he had known of the afternoon only that the wind whined in the roof and that the rain dripped through on to his back at intervals. When the sun at last stepped in between the banks of dung he could see that it was a forward spring. For his eye travelled up between the green walls of the road to the hills four miles away, and there the beech trees were almost in perfect leaf and in their dense ranks resembled a flock of sheep with golden fleeces descending the slope. Yet it wanted a week before May-day. The grass was good, and already the cows were clean and bright after their winter in the yard; and, having looked at his hands alongside the white and strawberry hide of the cow, he got up and wiped them on a wisp of grass beside the door. He stood there a moment - a tall, crooked man, with ever-sparkling eyes in a nubbly and bony head, worn down by sun and toil and calamity to nothing but a stone, hollowed and grey, to which his short black hair clung like moss; in his starved fields you might have found a weathered flint of the same shape, and have said that it was much like a man's head. He stretched himself, and then turned and called the cow by her name in a voice so deep and powerful that it was as if the whole shed and not a man's chest had uttered it.

He sat down again to milk and to think, with his face turned to the sun. He was thinking of the farmhouse under those woodson the hill, where he used to go courting twenty years ago, and of the girl, the only daughter of that house, who was now his wife. He had driven over there one day in his father's cart to see about some pigs. The old man had given him supper, hone and bread and butter, cold apple dumplings with cheese, and cowslip wine. It was a wonderful quiet house, very dark under tall beeches, with a quality in the dark still air as if it were under water, but very clean and bright with china and brass and the white tablecloth and the old man's white beard and glittering blue eyes. He knew that the old man was failing to make both ends meet, but there was no sign of it, and he spoke with a cheerful gravity, and there was a look about house and man as if they were apart from the world, and not subject to such accidents as failure of crops, cattle disease, and the like. They had done their business, and at the end of a long silence he was thinking of rising to go, when Emily, the daughter, came in without noticing him, kissed her father, and said, "Father, there is a white bird in the old apple tree of the rickyard singing like a blackbird. Yet 'tis as white as milk."

"Well, we will all come and see," said the old man, and then she saw that a stranger was there, and with a blush she retreated and opened the door. As she was shutting it she turned round out of curiosity, thus revealing her own face to the stranger, but seeing nothing of his which was in shadow. In a minute or two they went out into the rickyard where the cart was waiting. Emily was patting the horse's neck, but with her face towards the old apple-tree where a white blackbird was singing from the top-most branch. "You will not let them shoot it, father, will you?" she said. The white bird and its song, the girl's fair hair, and rosy face very serious, the unbent old man soon to die, the sombre smouldering old tiles and brick wall of the house, and the high black woods behind, were remembered now. Soon afterwards he had returned to the house, and again and again, avowedly to see Emily. In the late summer they used to walk out after the haymaking was all over, while the nightjar sang and the woods were dark and discreet and the sky above them as pale green as a new-mown field. They went in amongst the untrodden bracken together. He could recall the smell of the crushed fronds where they sat, the light of the near planet between the fox-gloves gushing from the violet sky, and the kisses that were as sweet as the honeysuckle overhanging them, and, un-like that, could be tasted again and again without cloying.

And now the cold whine of the wind in the roof and the drop of the rain, and Emily was lying at home, sick, with a dead new-born child in the next room, and a child that he was glad was dead, yes! that even she would not be cry-ing after if she knew what a monstrous mistaken thing had come into the world with their help. Weekes looked at that old farmhouse and the rickyard, the crushed bracken bow-er, as if to search among these things engraved by joy upon his brain for the devilish magic that had brought about this wretchedness. He looked at her remembered face, scan-ning it for something to explain this thing, looked closely and fiercely at the face that was turned back towards him in her father's doorway so that he loved her from that day. What? Why? But neither in the young girl nor in the worn woman could he see what he sought. He thought of their labours, of the six children she had borne and reared, of her rough hands and wrenched voice, of the smearing out of all her prettiness except her hair. He turned it over and over, ruminating, undisturbed by the spurting of the milk into the pail, the trickle of the shower, or the sight of the hills and the clouds over the hills. Yet he did not take his eyes off these hills, nor change the look given to them by his pain and questioning - questioning he knew not what now - the whole order of things, perhaps, from which the terror had sprung unexpected. Having naught for his brain to grip and hold, but only the dead ghastly child lying still, and repeating the question, and round about it the moving world of men and Nature, enormous and endless and careless, each effort was weaker than the last and sorrow brought its narcotic stupidity. It was some time after he had drawn her last milk that the cow licked his face impatiently. He kicked away the stool and began singing a verse of a ribald song which he did not know he had remembered -

> Poor Sally's face is plain
> But Sally's heart is kind

And it was so singing that, without wishing it, he returned the question to the teeming womb and grave of the earth, to be swallowed up in the vast profusion of life and death, while the merry maid waved to and fro the coloured silks of the sunshine and of the rain, and the titmouse crept through the hedge, crying, waggishly, "Fitchy! fitchy!"

SNOW AND SAND

The wind has as many voices as men have moods, and more. It can whimper like a child hiding alone. It can rave as if it was one of the gods of the early men, running wild in the night over a diminished world. It can whisper love and hate and satiety. It will breathe of doubt, apprehension, trepidation. Now it seems the youngest thing between earth and heaven, new made and fresh as bubbles on the brook. And now again it is an old wind. Hundreds of times it is an old wind, so old, that it has forgotten everything except that it is old and that all other things among which it wanders are young and have changed and will change; and it mumbles fitfully that what is young now will in a moment be old, and that to be old is nothing, nothing; and then in one breath it scatters the last handful of the dead tree's dust and flutters the first leaf of spring. While it covers up in sand the castle ruins that stood, like the two last teeth of an old hound, on a hillock above the sea, it thinks it was but yesterday that it unloosed the hair of the princess looking from the new-built tower of that castle towards the west. She sighs with fulness of beauty but ceases not to watch from the high window. The wind powders her hands and dulls her eyes with sea sand. She droops her eyelids yet looks still to the west. But now her eyes are fast shut and it is only her soul that can see through the milky blue lids of her blind eyes. The sand is hissing about her hair, but she cannot hear it; it is poured into the room like water. For the wind has filled itself with sand as but a little while before it filled itself with the gold of sunset and the scent of the rose; and the heavy billows of sand are drowning the sea-birds. The princess cannot hear the wrath of the sea any more than if she had eyes she could see it, through the sand storm, baying at the foot of the tower. She cannot feel the sand rising above her waist. She cannot cry out or fly; she has no desire or motion. There is not one left in the castle to cry out to her or to come to her door; for some have broken forth to die in the sea, and some have drunk the sand and have died like her amid the mist and hiss of the floating and whirling dunes. The tower plunges through the solid air into the black sea and buries the corpse of the betrothed. The wind blows her dust into my face as it shakes the drab grass on the last stones of the tower. It is an old wind. A minute ago it had forgotten such a little thing as the tempest of sand and sea, the overthrow of the tower, the maiden's death, and her black hair spread out by the slow wave. But now it has remembered as it whirls the sand and the crossing flakes of snow together, above the ruins of the tower, the drab grasses, the homeless dunes. There is nothing else to do but to remember here. It is a sea of solid waves, of sand hills that behold the mountains, the sea and the sky, and of sand valleys that behold only the sand hills and the sky. Some of the hills are stony grey or brown with dead bracken, some of the valleys yellow-green with moss and with moss-like turf, or grey with the sprawling roots and the flaked leaves of little willows. But most are bare of all but the corpse tresses of yellow grass, and the wind carves ceaselessly and erases its carving, and in small hollows bows the pointed stem of the grass and guides it so as to draw a circle upon the sand. Many skeletons of birds lie on the sand, but there is not a bird in the air, no sound but the shifting of the grains as the wind broods. There is nothing but change, unresting, monotonous change. The wind is counting the sands and going over memories which are as the sands. One hill is like the next and all the valleys are the same except one, wider and more level than the rest. It is paved with blue rippled water and on the water are myriads of pale birds that are sending up myriads to whirl and cry in the wind. The rushy margin is strewn with delicate bones and feathers among the snowflakes. The pale multitude rises and circles and descends and rises again to and from the solitary water. They are the souls of them who have loved nothing overmuch, who have lived on one another's breath and have floated hither and thither about another's business. They must keep together. They

73

are drawn to the waste pool among the dunes as in life they were drawn to nothing, and a footstep drives them away, to return inevitably again. They desire only not to be alone. I recognise many, and not one of them is strange. They never change. As they are to-day so they were when the maiden's tower was overwhelmed, and will be so long as there is water in the pool and safety and solitude around. Old men and young men and maidens, generation after generation, are indistinguishable in their grey and white plumage and wandering cries. They suffer a contentment that is not happiness. Their pale wings all together are beautiful. If they were not haunted by the living they might even be happy also, and float upon the water until they were weary, and then upon the wind until the water once more seemed better than the wind.

A few of them are still drifting overhead like larger snowflakes as I dip into the next valley, but in the next I am alone again among the sandhills, listening to the two gentle dissolving murmurs of the gliding sand and the kissing flakes, sounds that are taking possession of all things as of me, so that in all the drowsy world there seems nothing but the formless mazy snowfall and the vague changing dunes; and then, crossing a stream that flows among alders, in the fields between the dunes and the mountains, I find that I am upon a footpath hidden before but now revealed by the light snow lying close and pure white on the short grass or bare earth of its winding course. The water is full of yellow reeds, the catkins on the dark alders are blood red, the fields are very green, and the life in their longer grass has all but melted the snow. Already the light is fading from grass and reed and tree, and from the robin who, a moment ago, swelled an orange breast as he sang in the alder. He sings no longer but flits from the tree to the low stone wall of a garden that follows several loops of the stream. Between the water and the wall creeps the path, and on this path the robin suddenly appears, visible not in his flight but at the moment when he flutters before alighting. When he stands still I can hardly see him, and his black eye and hard ejaculated chirp emerge out of the dark air. But he seldom stands still. He flits ahead a few steps, or to one side, or to the wall, and from there to a branch, and back again, very suddenly and unexpectedly. He is more like the embodiment of a thought than a bird - coming thus out of darkness, announcing himself and disappearing again - a thought that is out of control and is living its own life, moving to some end which you cannot foresee though you may dread. Now I have eyes and ears only for this brown, shadowy, uncertainly moving thought that is one moment so still, another flickering, like a flame or a dead leaf. I watch for his movements, yet each one startles me. He enters a garden - the gate has rotted from its hinge - and I follow up a straight weedy path between thickets that were once vegetable plots; flowers of snow hang on the skeleton plants. Five stone steps lead up to a narrow door in a porch, with a window above it. On either side there are three windows one above the other in the old white wall, and on one side the dairy and sheds adjoin the house. The roof is thatched, and the porch and room above it have a roof of their own. A low stone chimney rises above the thatch at either end. It is certain that I have seen or known the house before this twilight.

House and garden are haunted. They are haunted by something quiet and small - by the robin and his gusty flight - by my thought - haunted by myself. I am the ghost in that snowy garden path outside the house, and my thought wanders helplessly about and around it like the white birds over the pool.

The house has never been unfamiliar to me. Since childhood it has been as clearly in my mind's eye - the seven windows, the door and the five steps, the garden on either side of the straight path up to the porch - as any house which my eyes have seen and my feet entered. Seven windows, seven eyeless sockets where there had been eyes.

A little time ago, ninety years, when the birds were flying up and down over the dunes, a bridegroom and bride had come home to that dark door on an evening of February. Ninety years ago the robin ceased singing and flickered about the path, and up the path towards the newly painted white house with bridegroom and bride. Ninety years ago a thought haunted them as now I am haunting the silent house; it may have been the same thought. The difference between the living and the dead is little at such times; there may be no real difference. My uncontrolled thought, born without any wish of mine, is chirping and flitting there on the path, or is gathered up into the twilight gusts in which sea-birds are wailing. At the top of the steps a man pauses, a tall pale man, black-haired, copper-bearded, dressed as a farmer should be who has just been married and has ridden home with his bride; he turns and looks over the dunes and then to the mountains above the curve of the bay, with a look as of one to whom the scene is familiar and yet foreign; that he was not born between the mountains and the dunes, and has not spent his childhood there, is clear from his uncomprehending and restless eyes. The small fair-haired woman at his side, well wrapped against the snow, looks so happy and at ease, while taking the same brief slow glance, that it may easily be known she is not so blessed by her marriage but that she is glad of a further blessing from this native coast. The wheeling birds complete her sense of the beauty of the day and the hour, the mountains, the dunes, and the sea, while they carry her husband's thought away, so that for a moment he is lost, lingering after she has passed into the house and not seeing the robin on the step below, my ghost in the path. Having looked long, too long, he follows his bride through the dark door. No light appears, and when he has gone I can no longer see the robin, and I hear only the shivering of the seedless dead stalks in the garden. My thought has gone in after those two. I stare at the windows behind which it has followed them. The door is closed. My thought is pleading with them, troubling them, as the robin, so restless and quick and then suddenly still, troubled me. It is troubling them, this little thought of the unborn, of one who is to come after them when they are in their graves. Can they in that solitary house foresee anything from the wheeling of the birds, the mazy fall of the snow, the rustling grass, the flickering flight and talk of the robin at the gate? A window is lit up and I see them seated together - he with bowed head watching her hands, which he is holding in his own over his knees; she looking straight out towards where I stand. She is silent while he speaks. He is reminding her that the farm is now his for ever, that they are not now any more just two persons content with one another, but two in the perhaps endless chain of destiny. He foresees the day when the land will be improved and a new house built to take the place of the old farm-stead that belongs to the old times, the old ways now passing; he is almost ashamed to bring her to the old place, but he will give up wandering now, he will be able to save, and their children will be better off than they are now, and their children's children. . . . He is talking to himself a moment. Then he says he half wishes he had taken her to his own land. He can never be quite at peace with all these barren sands at the edge of the land, and all those useless birds roving about the sand and the sky. Hark! They will not end their clamour. He takes down his gun from over the fire and goes out, and stepping swiftly over the dunes reaches the pool and fires into the multitude. They scream as if the firmament had a myriad voices and all of misery. They wheel about him as if they would lift him up in their anguished rush. The air is of wings. And in the house she hides her eyes from nothing, and waits. She smiles at his return. He drops a white bird into her lap and she smiles no more; nor yet does she reproach him, though she will not look at him, while she tells him the tradition among her father's people - that those birds are the spirits of the men and women who were buried in the sand hundreds of years ago. She says that she can think of nothing sweeter than to hover as a spirit over the pool near where she was born, and where perhaps her children will be keeping sheep and ploughing the good land and cutting fern from the mountain and gathering whinberries, for ever. She takes up the bird in her two hands, setting free her wrists from his, and says that some day, who knows, she will be like that and so will her children and children's children, flying and floating about their native land and ocean. She wipes the crimson from the white breast with her handkerchief. But he says that he will never be one of the long-winged homeless creatures that threaten to alarm their embrace, but rather a robin that likes men and the houses of men - 'Do not sigh, my wild, beautiful, white bird.' Is that the robin still loitering outside the window, he wonders. He rises and presses his face against the pane and sees me not. He is troubled by the white wings in his mistress' lap and the calling of its companions. He draws the curtains close over the window and shuts out all that he can of the haunting night, the soft-fingered snow, and me, and whatever in that altogether white world might prey upon those two even in their sleep.

AT A COTTAGE DOOR

The cottage was built upon the rock which just there protruded from the earth; and which was the rock and which the rough stone of the walls could not easily be told, so rude was the structure and so neatly was it whitened from the low eaves down to the soil. The threshold was whitened, so also were the stones of the path, the low wall in front, and several huge fragments here and there both within and without the gate. These white stones served instead of flowers. Other ornaments outside there were not, except stonecrop on the garden wall and at the sides of the threshold flagstone, a tall solitary spire of yellow mullein growing out of the top of the garden wall, and on the thatch itself a young elder tree against the white chimney stump, and an archipelago of darkest green moss which was about to become a solid continent and to obliterate the straw. Thatch and moss beetled over the walls which were pierced by two small windows of diamond panes. The chief light, when the door between these windows was shut, came from the fire-place which, with its iron and brasswork and the door of the brick oven adjacent, nearly filled one side of the living room. But the door was nearly always open, revealing most of the dark cave within, its red flameless fire, its bright knobs and bars of iron and brass, and the polished odds and ends of copper and brass on the mantelpiece or hanging on the wall - candlesticks, snuffers, horse-trappings, a gill measure, part of an old pair of scales, a small shell from a Boer battlefield.

The cottage must have been built before the road was made, or the roadmakers had omitted to notice it; for it lay back a hundred yards from the high hedge on top of a wall, through which a stile led over a rough meadow, between almost solid hillocks of brambles and clusters of royal fern under alder trees, to the white wall, the white stones, the cabbage plot and the white house itself. To a passing child it appeared that the cottage had originally been built in the heart of a stony wood; gradually the larger number of the trees had been cut down, thus exposing the cottage to someone on the road who had then been inspired to cut through the hedge and its wall, to cross the field, to drive out the savage or fairy inhabitants, and to take possession of it. In the field there were still great butts of oak visible, and on the further side of the house, showing above the chimney, were three dead trees close together raising a few shortened, stripped, and rigid pale arms to the sky and to deities who had long ago deserted them, the house and the surrounding land of small fields as rough as a windy sea, stone walls, hedges of aspen, oak and ash, rocky rises clothed lightly in oaks of snaky and slender growth, and beyond and above, on all sides but one, hills so covered with loose silvern crags among their bracken and birch that they resembled enormous cairns - where perhaps those deities had been buried under loads sufficient to keep them dungeoned away from any chance of meddling with a changed world.

In the cottage lived a mother and son. She was very little and very old. Her hair was still dark brown, her eyes almost as dark, her skin not quite so dark as her eyes, a nut-brown woman, lean, sweet, and wholesome-looking as a nut. She might often be seen sitting and looking to the south-west when a gap in the hills framed a vision of mountain peaks twenty miles beyond; and always she smiled a little. A passer-by might have thought that she never did anything but sit inside or outside the open door unless he had noticed the whiteness of the stones and the polish on the metal in the room where she had for fifty years collected things that could be polished. Few ever saw Catherine Anne at work save her son, and he not often, for he was away early and home late. He left her entirely alone, visited of none unless on days when the smart tradesman strode up the path, deposited her weekly packages on the table while he commented on the weather, and then replacing his pencil behind his ear bade her "Good Afternoon" in English. It was one of the few English remarks to which she could reply in English. Her only other English words were "beautiful" and "excursion train." For though some of the brown in her face was a gift of tropic suns in the days when she sailed with her husband on his ship, she had learned nothing but Welsh. The old man, so she called him though dead these forty years, had been against her learning English. A God-knowing and God-fearing Methodist, he had seen in that tongue the avenue through which his beautiful young wife might receive the knowledge of good and evil. After his death at sea she had of her own accord refused all contact with the thing, and now when it was all around her she never moved from the house. Her son knew it, but at home he spoke the native idiom, and when she heard him she seemed to be once more in her father's house, or in the orchard where little red apples overhung the rocky brook at the mountain foot. There it was that she gained, no one knows how, the nourishment from mother earth that gave her the deep contentment expressed in her health and her smile, in the shining metal, and in her patience - which was not endurance or torpor - patience of an order that seemed to be all but extinct in the world. Memory and hope were at balance in the brain that looked out of her brown eyes, and the present moment, often dull-seeming or even unkind, did not exist for her. Those eyes never closed while she sat by her door, and it might be conjectured that as she gazed east and north and west she saw more than the white stones and yellow stonecrop, the alders and royal fern, the hedge following the road, the lean oak trees among the rocks, the farther hills and their curlews and cairns, the sky, and now and then the uttermost mountains, which were all that an observer could see. If the casual observer waited more than a few moments in summer he might see that she was never quite alone. The air between her and the hills was the playground of several pairs of black swifts, wheeling and leaping round and up and down and straight forward, so that the bluest sky was never blank or the brightest grass without a shadow. Out of these birds two often screamed down precipitously to the white cottage and disappeared in their nests under the thatch above her head. Catherine Anne smiled a little more at these sudden stormy visits, and there were times when it seemed certain that she received others, though neither visible nor audible.

Some thought that she believed the swifts to be some kind of spirits, and one who was very wise said that if Catherine Anne Jones had been cleverer she might have been a wicked woman.

All the other swifts lived in the church. These had singled out her roof. They always returned to her; they had been there, ever since she came, every summer, singling that little place out of the whole earth and sky. She saw them high and swift and wild in the blue, and then she felt the flutter of their wings as they arrived at the eaves, and heard their soft talk together in the darkness. On summer evenings she saw them ascend into the heavens and not return, as blessed spirits might do; only on the morrow they were back again. They were always young, always equally dashing and joyous. It was whispered that she believed them to be the souls of her two children that died as babes, and they had come to her soon after the loss. "They were too young to know what to do in Heaven," she was reported to have said, "and so they were allowed to play about in Wales all the summer. But at night they have to return to see if they are wanted. Blessed birds. I daresay all birds are good if we only knew. I suppose I am too old to be one, but if it were lawful I should like nothing better than to live like them, passing the time until Judgment Day. What a lot of people there will be there to be sure - there were over three hundred in my native place when I was a girl, and I don't think there is one alive but me. I think some ought to be birds. Birds take up so little room, and they could not do any mischief if they wanted to. Now, if only the town people were all to be turned into birds. Lord, such a fright I had two years ago last February. I was sitting here, it being fine, to see the sun rise, and up from the town came a swarm of wings as many as there are leaves in yonder wood, small dark birds all close together and making a whistling noise, and I thought to myself, It has happened after all; they have changed all the people into blessed birds. No, I was not afraid about my son, for, thought I, now he will not be able to drink anything but cold water, and perhaps he will come to live in the church. I was glad. I thought of taking a walk down there just to see how the place looked, when along came the Insurance man - He isn't a bird, I thought to myself - and says: 'Are you looking at the starlings, mam?' 'No,' says I, and I was vexed. Dear me, all those birds was a beautiful sight, and such a nice noise they made between them as if they were glad to be going away from that place. It is a funny thing about birds, how different they are. Mrs Williams said to me once when she was courting, 'Why, Mrs Jones there are several kinds of birds.' Several! There are as many different kinds as there are men, and that is saying a lot, and remember I have sailed over the ocean five years and went ashore in all the ports of this mortal world. They are like people, only they don't seem to do any harm. Nice things! I used to think they must be very good not to be jealous of us having all the houses and food and things, but if people only knew they would be jealous of the birds. They are all different, or else how could He know when any one of the sparrows falls to the ground. They don't know what it is to be idle or too busy, nor the difference between work and play. There are not any rich and poor, and they respect one another. They are not all tangled up and darkened with a number of things. Then look how few of them die - did you ever see a dead bird? - except men shoot them. The reason is, they are good enough for Heaven as they are, so up they go like the dew when we are not looking."

It was not entirely due to the position of her front door that she always looked north or east or west, and chiefly west. From the back door her son's feet had worn a path which could be seen winding south over several fields until it was lost, by the next cottage, in another road, also going south, towards "that place."

She considered herself on the edge of the town, but still distinctly out of it. The next cottage, where the footpath joined the road, was in the town, so she thought; yet there was no outward sign of it unless that its low walls were not as clean, nor its brass so plentiful and so bright, and that its door, facing south, was often shut, and always when the wind was from that quarter.

From Catherine Anne's back door could be seen the roof and part of the wall of this cottage, another exactly like it a little beyond, then a cluster, including one not of whitened native stone, but of red brick and black mortar. All these were on the road. On either side of it, southward, there was a farm or two, white, but with sheds of corrugated iron that rattled under the mist drops from the ash trees embracing the group. From these farmyards the geese strutted across wet meadows in a line as if setting out on a long voyage. Beyond, the rough land sank, hiding all but the smoke of yet more houses in a hollow, and rose again to an unbroken line of slate roofs and dirty white walls, cutting into the bases of snowy cloud mountains whose look told that underneath them was the sea. Similar houses in irregular lines and groups, were dotted on the treeless fields to the east and west of this main line. These were the first houses of the town and they were not a mile from the cottage. Beyond them the land fell away but rose again after several lesser rises and falls into great hills whose tops commanded the sea to the south and east and, on the clearer Sundays of the year, the same mountains as Catherine Anne's front door. These concealed rises and falls, and the slopes of the great hills, were the town.

From the brink, where that unbroken line of roofs notched the white clouds with its chimneys, the whole town could be seen. Over this brink fell the southward road and with it lesser roads which soon branched and multiplied into the mass of the town which choked the valleys as if it had slid down the hills in avalanches. The hills formed almost a circle, broken only by a gap on either side letting in the river from the mountains and out to the sea. Thus the town sprawled over the sides of a rudely carven bowl with deeply scalloped edges and with a bottom flat nowhere save at the narrow strip around the stream. The summits of these hills were clear of houses, and great expanses of their sides, though obviously conquered by the town, were still virgin and green and strewn with great stones.

Two of the hills on one side, that farthest from the stream, were not marked by a single street. Of these one, the highest of all, was clothed in grass from foot to ridge except on a broad lap which it made halfway up, and on that there was a house standing at the edge of a field sometimes golden with corn, and divided from it by a clump of black firs. The house was huge, both tall and wide, grey and square, with many windows towards the sea lighted only at sunset and that by the last beams in which a score of them blazed together. No road was seen climbing the steep slope to the house or leaving it for the ridge above. Some poet or haughty extravagant prince must have built it there inaccessibly with windows for the great town, the sea, the mountains. It was sombre and menacing. It was empty. It scorned the town. In its turn the town had left it up there to perish like an eagle upon a mountain ledge, shot by the hunter, but out of his reach. The neighbour hill was not so high, but it was bare not only of houses but of grass and

corn and every green thing, and its only trees stood near
the summit, leafless and birdless, stark and pale as if newly
disinterred from an ancient grave. They were being slowly
buried by the brown and fatal refuse - scarred deeply by
rains and by ever new cataracts of the same substance -
which covered and largely composed this hill. Out of its
summit stuck a chimney and round it the black figures of
men came and went against the sky. At the foot were other
chimneys, gigantic and black, and below them black buildings whose windows glowed night and day with fire such as
the old house had for a few moments at sunset. The smoke
mingled with white rain, and mist wreathed wildly about
the brown and the green hill.

Through the river's entry below these chimneys might
be seen other hills that sent down tributaries to its waters,
green hills with ravines of oaks and one or two white farms,
and far beyond these, more like the dream of a dreamer
than rock and peat, the abode of raven, buzzard and badg-
er, of freedom and health - the mountains of the source of
the river.

The stream itself, in the midst of the town, was a black
and at times a yellow serpent in a cage of steep iron-bound
banks, watched by furnace, store-house, and factory. It was
allowed a mock liberty only to stray into other cages of
steep-sided wharves. The blackened labourer stood on the

edge and spat at it where it writhed deep below. A careless child or a desperate man was engulfed by it on some night of fire and blackness, but it remained sullen and regarded not the trivial offering. The embrace with the sea was licensed, bridled, sternly watched by tall cranes, a hundred ships, and the long bleached spine of a breakwater where sea-faring men, idlers, and fluttering girls walked up and down.

The courses of the avalanches from the opposite hills were marked by white, dirty white, grey, and all but black, belts of houses broadening out to the mass in the valley. At the broad brow of the hills, in sight of the sea and of violet hills across the sea, a few farm-houses and their outbuildings still shone, while others mouldered grey and aghast and without tenants. Some of their fields were still left between the streets, but their barbed wire and patched hedgerows and walls imprisoned only an old horse or two, a temporary flock of sheep or of lean American steers on their way to the slaughterhouse and the tables of the town; and even where there were no houses straight lines of streets were waiting to be built along. Across this tainted and condemned grass, even between the houses, trotted narrow brooklets over stony beds to their sepulchres in the town sewers. The houses on the upper slopes were like Catherine Anne's, though most were slated, not thatched.

Fowls stalked or scuttered round about and through the open doors. The gardens were walled with once whitened stones and contained a few twisted apple trees. Old women of a former age stood on the doorsteps or moved busily in scanty undress, bareheaded. Old men pottered about, or leaned on their spades to talk or look out to sea or at the pigs. The smell of baking bread was blown from the doors. Their furniture, their Bible and theological works, were old. The curs were descended from sheep dogs that once herded the mountain flocks on these slopes. The road was still a watercourse, and the unnecessary tradesman could hardly ascend if he wished, except on foot. There was always a robin in the roadway, a wagtail in the glittering streamlet, often a rook on the square stone chimney, look-ing down at the town as if his ancestors had told him that it was new and might disappear any night - but as he saw that nothing was likely to happen immediately he turned his head, hopped into the air, and flew away over the hilltop.

The streets beginning on the hill-ridge ended in the thickest of the town, in a medley of steep criss-cross streets interrupted here and there by black squares of workshops with ever-burning furnaces and ever-smoking chimneys. Here every inch of the soil was covered with bricks, stones, cement, asphalte, iron-work, granite blocks. Not a tree or blade of grass was allowed to appear anywhere but in the graveyards, and even there the earth was plated almost entirely with tombstones. They were afraid of leaving any space unguarded lest Nature should show a regret, a curse or a warning. The river was unsightly, but must be tolerated alternately with insult and respect. But even here there was not an end of the "country." Through many open doors could be seen furniture like Catherine Anne's, and old women of her period. Thousands passed them many times a day, but they were built in days when everyone knew everyone else, and so the doors were still left open while the baking and the washing were done. The drunkard stumbled out of the crowd into the warm and rustic seclusion of his home. The child rushed out from the cradle he was tending and was swept along by the procession to meals or work. Women stood at doorways and talked, while one went on with her knitting or suckled her babe. A half-naked child wriggled through the crowd carrying tins of dough, for if they could not bake, at least they would knead and leaven their bread, at home. Many of the children were bare-legged and headed, dirty, hungry, and quick. Out of one or other of the houses would come a bent woman, wrinkled and foul, holding a shawl over her head, looking as if she had spent a thousand years in the cellar, crushed down in rigid, idle suffering like a toad embedded in an oak root. Such creatures, chiefly women, were not uncommon. They were small, grey-skinned, with clotted grey hair; they had scarred faces, had lost an eye and most of their teeth; they wore soiled print or black dresses, bedraggled like the plumage of a dead bird in the mud and in colour approaching the foul dust of the pavement and the garbage of the gutter. In appearance they were genuine autochthons. This earth of flagstone, asphalte, granite, brick, iron, and ashes, might have protruded such a monstrous birth on a night of frost, to prove that it was not yet barren in its age and ignominy. One such crone crawling out into the light, unclean, dull and yet surprised, had a look as if she had just been exhumed; she might have been buried alive in the foundation of the town for luck, and had now emerged to see what had been done. They were seen outside the taverns with their hands hidden under the remains of aprons, or were questing in the dustbins for food or unbroken glass; often they carried babies in whose shapeless faces was hidden the power to excel their grandmothers. When they were drunk in an alley a crowd of labourers and shopkeepers gathered to watch their waving arms and poisonous faces and hear their blazing curses screeched against some unlucky man. "There will be murder," said one. "It is a shame that such things are allowed," said another. None dared to enter the mouth of the alley. The crowd recognised that a different species, a chance-begotten, mis-delivered, and curse-nourished spawn of humanity was living side by side with them, farther removed than slaves or domestic animals. It was sometimes proposed that if the streets were kept cleaner and the sewage improved this race might vanish, as if in fact it ate filth and lived in the drains. No one dared to interfere. Presently a woman rushed after the man into a house, and the door was slammed with a sound not of wood but of flesh and bone.

Such were not numerous; the majority were genuine villagers, but the minority was representative and it alone truly belonged to the place. They were villagers with a difference. One face expressed nothing but the abstraction caused by solitude in the midst of myriads. The next smiled with the intimacy of home or inn. Few had yet quite realised that they were living not at the edge of a field but in the bowels of a town, though most days it was impossible to hang clothes out to dry in the flagged or asphalted or trodden mud yards, since the air was so foul that it was worth while buying the head of a sheep fed in the neighbourhood for the sake of the copper in its teeth. Every house beheld chimneys and furnaces from one window, from another the masts of the docks or the sea and its little sails or the brown and the green hill side by side, over the ploughed sea of slate roofs. On pleasant days the smell of the sea, modified by the docks, mingled with the acrid smell and taste of smoke from the smelting of copper or the burning of carcases for manure; but at night either smell was drowned in that of fried fish. Every other house had a large window to expose fruit, vegetables, groceries, meat, "herbal remedies," and above all fried fish, for sale. Every corner house was a tavern, its windows foul with breath and steam within and mud, rain, and fine ashes without. The houses were small, so that tavern and church and school were conspicuously islanded among the low roofs.

But, towards the river, away from the avalanches of buildings, the houses were high and supported on plate glass windows of immense size. The streets curved and doubled after a pattern created centuries ago by the neighbourhood of a castle whose Norman masonry was still hiding in fragments behind or within some of the shops. Inns and shops were old but with glittering new faces of glass, stone, ornamented tiles, and vast gold letters. The wires of telegraph, telephone, and electric light ran amongst and over antique stone and timber work. Every inch was obviously designed or converted to serve an immediate purpose; there was no largeness, no waste, nothing haphazard, no detail forgotten through the pursuit of some ideal; all was haste, grim and yet slatternly. Here and there an old house had been pulled down, and its place hidden by a temporary wooden fence, stuck over with advertisements in black, white, crimson, and blue, of drugs, infant foods, political meetings, auction sales, corsets, men's clothes, theatres - these last showing beauteous dishevelled adulteresses and heroic gentlemen in white shirts threatening them with revolvers - men in diving costume fighting for a bag of jewels at the bottom of the sea. Everywhere the ideal implicit was that of a London suburb. The shop walker came nearest to achieving this ideal: suave and superb in dress, manner, and speech, in all but salary, he had been metamorphosed from the son of a farmer, who spoke no English, into an effigy that put to shame the Pall Mall clubman, though he cost the nation incomparably less. Pity that he had so poor a world to shine in, and that his imitators resembled him no more than they did the figures exhibited in the tailor's advertisements, figures created merely to hold a cigarette between the lips and a whippy cane in the fingers. His clients included women bent on dressing extravagantly or even with aristocratic sumptuous modesty, at a low price; young men with white faces, riding breeches, cigarettes, and jaunty manners; sober farmers who had tired of wearing the same old homespun so thick that they shiver without it; wives who have come to town to sell butter and eggs; sailors who have just found a ship, sailors who have just been paid off, sailors who have called first at "The Talbot Arms"; dark-eyed, clear-complexioned girls swaddled in blouses of red and black chequered flannel, blue and white flannel skirts, variegated or black and red flannel shawls, but, for all their natural and artificial plumpness, gay and continually chattering in musical voices as they move quickly about carrying well-scoured buckets of white wood on head or hips - women resembling wood-pigeons in their plumpness and quickness. All were buying what was very cheap, or very showy, or very new, or very much like something else, or much praised as a really good thing. Cattle and their drovers looked in at the gorgeous windows and spread over the streets where a dozen knots of old acquaintances were meeting for the first time since last market day. Young working men in black whose faces had clearly been of another colour recently but were now very white by contrast with dark eyes and black moustaches and hair, walked up and down the pavements doing nothing in a determined fashion and smoking, - men who might easily have been changed into starlings in an age of miracles. In nearly all, in men and women - except in the squalid hooded hags who crawled by, or the work girls beside them carrying younger sisters or bastards in shawls - the pallor, stiffness, and haste of the town were modified by country ways, a rolling walk as if on solitary roads, country gestures and speech and quiet eyes. Young and old of all classes mingled on an equality. There was no inharmonious element, it was a village crowd, and all were united by the fact that they had been peasant born and that they were now slaves to the town. They were fascinated by the charm of the town, which is, that it is there easy to fill the whole of life with a rapidly changing round of duties and necessities, where shops and all things are so convenient that life, as Catherine Anne had surmised, is swallowed up by its conveniences.

At one end of the glassy street the opposing cliffs of the house walls framed a portion of the brown burning mountain and white clouds standing above it; at the other end, under a railway arch, was a maze of gulls swaying between the steady masts of ships.

In and out of the crowd, relentless but polite, and turning round corners, passing one another, climbing this way and that the hills of the town, went the electric trams. They were polished, compact, efficient, without limbs. Like the machinery in the factories they must be of the best material and kept bright and oiled. They were tended like idols and altars with hate and fear that resembled love in its extremity. Men and women might be maimed, deformed, decrepit, pale, starved, rotten, but the wheels, the brakes, the brass-work, the advertisements, and the glass windows must be continually inspected and without spot.

Two girls of seventeen or eighteen, fair-haired - just so

tall that one who cared would have said, Even so tall ought women to be - straight, quick, and graceful as mountain sheep, walked down a bye street beside the tram. They wore newly washed gay cheap gowns. Their heads were bare and their yellow hair drew down the sunlight. Their clear, rosy, small-featured faces were fresh and full of a boyish confidence - like boys among a crowd who are all companions. Their full, parted lips wavered and disclosed perfect teeth as they smiled and talked. The exquisite balance of their heads might have been called arrogant if it had not been careless and unaffected by the admiration, curiosity, and scorn of the crowd. Sometimes they held one another's hands as if unconsciously fearful of the town. It was easy to imagine these two changed into such birds of the sea-shore as terns, bright of wing and foot, for ever flitting in the sun and spray with merriment, speed and grace, and without care. They belonged to some wandering family encamped for a fair near by. A chauffeur rubbed the metal of his lamp till it flashed. There was no one to take care of these two. Instead, the town surged high above and around them to destroy them if it could, to force them to suckle gnomes at their delicate breasts.

Beyond these restless streets rose other hills away from the docks into unpolluted sea air. The town spread up on to the sides of these - first long rows of new clean houses of one pattern and few shops; above them long terraces of houses of many forms, with gardens, shrubberies, oak trees; and still higher isolated large houses hidden by foliage, where parties played croquet and the solitary lounged with a book among flowering bushes and looked at the sea. The windy crest was free, and the half-made road ended in a deep overgrown track, now half a wood, down which the men of the mountains used to descend to the river and the ships and the sea. The oaks here were but young, yet they were stony and twisted and gaunt with the sap of other trees, stony and twisted and gaunt, that were descended from those through which the ancient men had their first glimpse of the river mouth, the small ships and the fires of their adversaries, before they plunged downward silently. Now between those twisted stems the eyes looked one way over the town to the white walls of Catherine Anne's cottage, the woods, the lesser hills, the great mountains so far away and pure that the breast heaved an involuntary sigh; the other way, in the gathering darkness, at a pale half moon of sea bounded just below by a curve of lamps low down as far as the docks, and then by the cloudy forms of hills with lights like stars upon their sides.

But at night the town irresistibly confined the gaze. It was a pit glittering with distinct small lights and glowing with the orange and scarlet furnaces that seemed to have eaten large squares out of the streets. Beyond, based in fire, the brown hill and the green hill rose indistinguishably dark into the midst of the stars. The pit was sounding with clanking and humming noises that recorded the activity of a demon, not of men, for not a whisper was heard of footsteps, voices, blows, caresses, of the love, anger, fear, anxiety, thought, argument, confusion, of men and women. It was impossible to remember that down there slept or waked those thousands of dark men, the mixed multitude, the buxom cocklewomen like wood pigeons, those two fair ones like terns. The demon was humanity, a demon not born of woman, whose right hand knows not the deed of its left hand, though every nerve in its frame is a twitching soul. It knows not and recks not what it is making, as it squats there upon the earth. It feeds upon itself day and night, loading an immeasurable craw and looking up with small eyes on the sun and stars as senselessly as they look down upon it. It is cruel in ignorance, it is pitiful, and it forgets. It is hideous and beautiful. It would be noble but it must be vile. It is winged but cannot rise, so many are the claws that grapple into the earth. It is old but it is as a babe. But at this hour of night the pity and the vileness, the power and the beauty of it were under a veil. It crouched motionless, its bright eyes looked up, and the stars looked back, neither understanding, nor any longer questioning.

Where Lay My Homeward Path

It sang and knew not what it sang. Down there in the glimmering darkness, the demon sang, and through the obscurity of the song pierced the burden - that, with the river by which it is seated, and the mountain standing by, and the sea knocking without, and the ceiling of stars, it had a common birth; that their seeming strife is but the rude play of giant children nursed together and destined to one end; that the grass is waiting to grow upon it as upon the hills and the the wreckage of fallen stars, and fire waiting to consume the grass, and the fire to burn itself out; and that in the meantime life is an inspiration of matter and must sing and must also make themes for songs. So that it resembled nothing so much as the old woman sitting at her cottage door and looking at the coming and going of the swifts from the eaves to heaven and from heaven back again, in a mystery.

THE STILE

Three roads meet in the midst of a little green without a house or the sign of one, and at one edge there is an oak copse with untrimmed hedges. One road goes east, another west, and the other north; southward goes a path known chiefly to lovers, and the stile which transfers them to it from the rushy turf is at a corner of the copse.

The country is low, rich in grass and small streams, mazily sub-divided by crooked hedgerows, with here and there tall oaks in broken lines or, round the farm houses, in musing protective clusters. It is walled in by hills on every side, the higher ones bare, the lower furred with trees, and so nearly level is it that, from any part of it, all these walls of hills, and their attendant clouds can be seen.

I have known the copse well for years. It holds an acre of oaks two or three generations old, the roots of ancient ones, and an undergrowth of hazel and brier which is nearly hidden by the high thorn hedge.

One day I stopped by the stile at the corner to say good-bye to a friend who had walked thus far with me. It was about half an hour after the sunset of a dry, hot day among the many wet ones in that July. We had been talking easily and warmly together, in such a way that there was no knowing whose was any one thought, because we were in electrical contact and each leapt to complete the other's words, just as if some poet had chosen to use the form of an eclogue and had made us the two shepherds who were to utter his mind through our dialogue. When he spoke I had already the same thing in the same words to express. When either of us spoke we were saying what we could not have said to any other man at any other time.

But as we reached the stile our tongues and our steps ceased together, and I was instantly aware of the silence through which our walking and talking had drawn a thin line up to this point. We had been going on without looking at one another in the twilight. Now we were face to face. We wished to go on speaking but could not. My eyes wandered to the rippled outline of the dark heavy hills against the sky, which was now pale and barred with the grey ribs of a delicate sunset. High up I saw Gemma; I even began trying to make out the bent star bow of which it is the centre. I saw the plain, now a vague dark sea of trees and hedges, where lay my homeward path. Again I looked at the face near me, and one of us said:

"The weather looks a little more settled."

The other replied: "I think it does."

I bent my head and tapped the toe of my shoe with my stick, wishing to speak, wishing to go, but aware of a strong unknown power which made speech impossible and yet was not violent enough to detach me altogether and at once from the man standing there. Again my gaze wandered dallying to the hills - to the sky and the increase of stars - the darkness of the next hedge - the rushy green, the pale roads and the faint thicket mist that was starred with glow-worms. The scent of the honeysuckles and all those hedges was in the moist air. Now and then a few unexpected, startled and startling words were spoken, and the silence drank them up as the sea drinks a few tears. But always my roving eyes returned from the sky, the hills, the plain to those other greenish eyes in the dusk, and then with a growing sense of rest and love to the copse waiting there, its indefinite cloud of leaves and branches and, above that, the outline of oak tops against the sky. It was very near. It was still, sombre, silent. It was vague and unfamiliar. I had forgotten that it was a copse and one that I had often seen before. White roses like mouths penetrated the mass of the hedge.

I found myself saying "good-bye." I heard the word "good-bye" spoken. It was a signal not of a parting but of a uniting. In spite of the unwillingness to be silent with my friend a moment before, a deep ease and confidence was mine underneath that unrest. I took one or two steps to the stile and, instead of crossing it I leaned upon the gate at one side. The confidence and ease deepened and darkened as if I also were like that still, sombre cloud that had been a copse, under the pale sky that was light without shedding light. I did not disturb the dark rest and beauty of the earth which had ceased to be ponderous, hard matter and had become itself cloudy or, as it is when the mind thinks of it, spiritual stuff, so that the glow-worms shone through it as stars through clouds. I found myself running without weariness or heaviness of the limbs through the soaked overhanging grass. I knew that I was more than the something which had been looking out all that day upon the visible earth and thinking and speaking and tasting friendship. Somewhere - close at hand in that rosy thicket or far off beyond the ribs of sunset - I was gathered up with an immortal company, where I and poet and lover and flower and cloud and star were equals, as all the little leaves were equal ruffling before the gusts, or sleeping and carved out of the silentness. And in that company I had learned that I am something which no fortune can touch, whether I be soon to die or long years away. Things will happen which will trample and pierce, but I shall go on, something that is here and there like the wind, something unconquerable, something not to be separated from the dark earth and the light sky, a strong citizen of infinity and eternity. The confidence and ease had become a deep joy; I knew that I could not do without the Infinite, nor the Infinite without me.